D1433067

Dark Corners

By Reuben "Tihi" Hayslett

Edited by Lisa Diane Kastner & Asam Ahmad

Text copyright © 2019 Running Wild Press

Published in North America and Europe by Running Wild Press. Visit Running Wild Press at www.runningwildpress.com Educators, librarians, book clubs (as well as the eternally curious), go to www.runningwildpress.com for teaching tools.

ISBN (pbk) 9781947041226
ISBN (ebook) 9781947041233

Library of Congress Control Number
Printed in the United States of America.

Forward

I first met Tihi in Washington, D.C. during a training for people who wanted to become digital organizers. We met briefly, but didn't really connect until four years and 3,000 miles later, both calling Long Beach, CA home.

Getting to know Tihi more over the past few months has been a pleasure and when Tihi asked me to write the foreword to his book, it wasn't hard to say yes. As I learned more about his history it becomes increasingly clear why his art connects with me.

Tihi is very different from the people in the professional world where we met; the digital space—even among progressives—is very white, male, and economically comfortable. As a first-generation American and Black woman, I related to the unique struggles of being a minoritized person in our professional community. I also see how the skill of working among and relating with people of different walks of life translates into how the characters remain relatable from story to story.

As a fellow digital organizer who uses their writing chops for their nine to five, I know how hard it is to take the time to create. Fortunately for us readers, Tihi made that time. Growing up as a young first-generation American, Black girl, I struggled to connect to most of the stories I saw in print and film. For a long time I thought the problem was me, but now as a thirty-something woman who now is well-versed in feminist theory and media literacy I know that the lack of connection said more about society as a whole than me as an individual. I hope the collection of these short stories will help more young people see themselves in literature.

Instead of the saccharine, friday-night TV families meant to conjure nostalgia for a time when (white) women stayed at home and children were seen, but never heard, this collection shows readers very real and complicated human beings.

In these increasingly politically polarizing times, it's more important than ever that we have media that reflects us, connects us, and reflects a commonality that can bring us together. Tihi does that. The core of the human condition is present in all of us and we can tell stories of different identities and peoples with respect and dignity.

It's pleasing to see such a diverse array characters be so presented in such a normal way. Each individual is not presented as a token, but rather just another human being who has some real life issues that are often rendered invisible.

I encourage anyone who is also sick of consuming media that is too male and too pale to grab this book. I believe there isn't a better time to be a Black creative. After you read these stories, I think you will, too.

Wagatwe Wanjuki, feminist writer and activist

Funkier Than A Mosquito's Tweeter

The Howard sisters weren't pretty. Sarah and Christine had buck teeth like white building blocks, capped off by wide noses, hoop nostrils and Alabama-black skin. Justin used to throw rocks at them while they walked to school and called them voodoo witches. They'd hold hands with their heads pointed down to the dirt road and step faster, trying to out-walk him. But Justin was fast and he wouldn't let up.

When they bloomed at twelve years old their Papa couldn't buy bras and large shirts fast enough to keep up with them and Justin kept throwing rocks, not on their way to school, but at night, tossing pebbles at their window while he propped himself up on a tree branch.

"Psst, Sarah!" he'd whisper-yell, "psst! Come on, Chrissy."

He wouldn't look either one in the eye in daytime. But he'd be outside every night on the tree they grew up dancing and playing around, shaking his fists around his chest and flicking his tongue whenever he got their attention.

One day on the walk to school the Howard sisters cornered Justin at a bend in the road.

"You wanna see our teets?" Sarah asked him.

"Come back tonight with three dead crickets." Christine said.

"And eat 'em in front of us." Sarah finished.

"You crazy bitches are voodoo!" Justin said, pushing past Sarah. "Y'all are going to hell!"

Justin broke out into a run the whole way to school. But that night

1

he was back in the tree, pebbles in one hand, dead crickets in the other. After he chewed them up Sarah squeezed her chest against the window and Justin leaned so far toward her he almost lost his balance on the branch.

The next day, on the way to school, Justin had three more dead crickets.

"Ew, we don't want no crickets!" Christine said.

"Get us lizard tails." Sarah said.

"Yeah, lizard tails," said Christine, "five of 'em."

And Justin was back that night.

After two weeks Sarah and Christine had run out of ideas for gross things Justin could eat; he munched on beetles, dragonflies, cockroaches and boll weevils. They rode with their Papa into town to visit the local library, for research. That night they had specific instructions for Justin. The eight dead grasshoppers were no longer good enough. Justin would now have to sift through cow manure on Ol' Willie's farm.

When he came back the next night, pressed tits against a window pane wouldn't cut it for all the literal shit Justin had gone through. He demanded inside. He demanded touching and no bras and both sisters, not just one or the other. They pushed the window open to the stiff winds of the late fall and used an old bed sheet to help Justin climb through. Inside he opened his hand, revealing the brown stained mushroom roots.

"Eat it!" Christine said.

"Eat it and we'll take off our shirts!" Sarah added. Their wide brown eyes brimmed.

The fungal matter slid rough down Justin's throat and he asked the girls to fetch him a glass of milk. As they crept slowly through the hall and down the stairs—careful not to wake Papa—Justin sat on Sarah's bed, staring out at the half moon. He lost track of time there looking at its craters and ridges; he could almost feel the texture of the moon's surface on his palms as he rubbed them back and forth across Sarah's pillow. He imagined the pillow felt like breasts, moving up and down against his touch, receding back and plumping around his fingers. The stars hanging up there with the moon pulsated too and then started to spin into round discs—round like the Howard sisters.

Justin's stomach churned and he took his eyes off the sky. But the stars followed like tiny comets streaming into the room and onto the bed—which now started to bobble up and down and back and forth the same way Justin would hump and thrust on his bed at night when he thought about Sarah and Christine, and their tits.

He felt his stomach spiral in knots and the night breeze slowly tilted his head to the side. Comet tails flowed round the room like thick water waves, like thick women's curves. He heard tapping footsteps outside the door and then Sarah and Christine tip toed in. Their pale eyes blinked against their black skin as they sat on Christine's bed, opposite him. They smiled at him and Justin saw comet tails stream out of their mouths and wrap around their faces, only they weren't comet tails when he squinted closer. Then he felt a shift in his ears and behind his eyes.

"Are you ready?" Sarah asked him, a thick black line slithered out of her mouth and into her nostril. Justin blinked and when he readjusted to the dark he saw that the comet tails were really lizard tails. The humps and waves of the air were roach wings flapping in slow motion. The moon's craters were black centipedes curled into round balls. And as Sarah and Christine lifted their shirts, their inside skin was crawling with beetles, scurrying under their clothes and retreating when they breached the white of their cotton bras.

"Voodoo!" Justin yelled. The sisters shushed him with contorted faces. Under the door a path of light struck from their Papa's bedroom, scaring back the scorpions hiding in the dark.

"Girls!" Their Papa called out as he stepped into the hallway. The shadow he cast phased into a preying mantis, long curved legs and thick curved arms stalking slowly forward. The girls threw their shirts on just as black moths fluttered out their sleeves.

The whole insect world pressed on Justin with the bulbous force of breasts against glass and he was trapped within it. He made a mad dash for the window, swatting his arms at the spiders and the fleas and the weevils until he fell all the way down to the bed of rocks he had once thrown.

2016

January

My bathroom doesn't have any ventilation except a window in the shower, but it's cold, so I don't risk it. I step out, grab the towel, and reach for the lotion when I "see" it. Dark spots around my eyes, except that's not entirely right. Two soft white dots are where my pupils should be. But it looks like they hover over me. I can still see my face, if I look through it. I wipe the mirror and it goes away.

I'm not even dressed yet when my sister texts me a picture of a pregnancy test. It's positive. I'm still naked, fumbling for my panties when the phone rings.

"OMG!" My sister talks in acronyms.

"Yeah, this is exciting! Congrats."

"You have to get over here. Right now."

"Let me get dressed."

"Girl, get your ass here. I need you."

My sister's husband is white. He works in finance but swears he's not destroying the world. Our parents don't care; he makes money. And if anyone is giving them grandchildren, it's Stasha.

I have to transfer from the A to the R to get to her. They live in a brownstone, but only own the first floor. When I get there, he answers, and squeezes me before I can unbutton my jacket.

"Dale!" He says, "This is... I can't even get the words."

"You're gonna be a father, Matt. That's big time." I tell him.

"Stasha's waiting for you."

I make it past the doorway once Matt stops hugging me. Take my coat off and Matt rushes it off. Stasha's in the den, sitting cross-legged on the sofa with the pregnancy test on a ceramic plate on the coffee table. Stasha's eyes are wider than usual, but she doesn't smile with teeth, more like a smug grin.

"Didn't you just pee on that?" I ask her.

"Shut up and come here."

We hug.

"I wanted you be here when we call Mom and Dad." Stasha says.

"Yeah okay."

The light from the windows behind her casts a glow around the hair she buys online and pays to get sewn into her scalp. She wants to video call our folks and I warn her about old people and technology. Matt has to troubleshoot our dad through it. Stasha won't move off the couch, even when I tell her the backlighting from the windows will block us out. Maybe our parents will see Matt.

"Stasha!" Our mom yells. "Is that you? I can't see you. Hello, Matt!"

"Dale's here too." Matt says.

"Oh okay, what's going on?"

"Hi Mom." I say.

Matt says, "Stasha's got some big news."

"You got promoted!" My mom says.

"No, better!" Stasha says, "where is it? Dale, pass it to me."

"Gross! No. Mom, where's Dad?"

"Making a sandwich."

We wait for Dad to finish even though he keeps saying to go ahead without him. We don't though. We wait until they're both sitting next to each other. We can see them but the sunlight behind us casts us all in shadow.

"Mom, Dad," Stasha gushes. "Matt and I are pregnant!" Then she screams, right in my ear.

Dad says, "Well, hot damn." And Mom says, "Yes! About time!"

We go through the usual questions: when did they find out? Just an hour ago. How long were they trying? They weren't really trying. Do they think it's a boy, anyone have fish dreams? No, no one.

My dad says, "how's my other baby girl doing?"

"I'm good, Daddy."

My mom asks, "do you still have dreads, Dale? I can't really see."

"Yes, Mom."

"They look terrible."

Daddy takes a bite of his sandwich and says, "Well, since the girls and Matt are here, we should tell them."

"Harold, no," Mom says, "we're not ruining Stasha's day."

"Ruin? What happened?" Stasha says.

"Tell us, Daddy." I say.

"So, it's still early," he says.

Mom interrupts him, "your father has cancer."

February

Bernie Sanders loses South Carolina and my white boss is shocked. I run social media for an organic, socially conscious juice company. My white boss arm-chair campaigns about what Bernie should have done differently, but he gets one thing right. Losing South Carolina isn't a good signal for the Black vote. He doesn't ask me about the Black vote.

At karaoke in Clinton Hill, I run into Leah. She says she broke up with her boyfriend and is done with men for good. I'm drunk so I believe her. We turn Tracy Chapman's "Fast Car" into a duet and go home together.

I'm in her shower, when I see it again, the halos over my eyes, I call her into the bathroom and ask her to look in the mirror with me.

"I don't see anything."

"You don't?" I say. "It's right there." I draw circles in the air over my eyes. The shadows seem bigger in her apartment. But I can still see past them, into my face.

"You're tripping," Leah says, "like all these new age gentrifying white girls up in here."

"I guess you should know. Did you meet a lot pretending to be straight with a white man?"

"That's not fair, Dale."

"I know, I'm sorry."

"Do you get jealous of men?" Leah asks me.

"Stop that," I say, "we're not doing that."

"Oh, so we're doing a séance instead?"

"I hate you."

I'm done in the shower, but Leah takes off her clothes and steps in.

March

Thank Beyonce, Stasha asks one of her sorority friends to plan the baby shower. But she calls me to dig up dirt on my sister.

"What are things only the two of you would know?"

"That our father has prostate cancer?" I deadpan.

"No, like real stuff. Something funny and embarrassing."

Stasha and Dad have doctor's appointments during the same week. Everything goes as expected: the baby is alive and healthy, my father is alive and dying.

I text my mom to ask how Dad's holding up and she replies, "fine," and texts me links to job postings in advertising.

April

The eye-halos are the biggest I've ever seen them the day after Prince dies. They're like tennis balls hovering over my eye sockets. The rest of my face "glows" a soft white, like a skull. I catch myself staring at it, wondering if a ghost is hovering over me, and when my phone rings, I vomit.

It's a text from Matt: "I just heard about Prince. Are you okay?"

I keep retching and wipe my face when I'm finished. The skull is still there.

From Matt: "I'm not sure if you're a fan or not. But I figured you might be. Drinks on me? Your sister says Hi."

Everyone wears purple at work, but I'm the only one my boss lets take the day off. Leah's inconsolable and won't leave her bed. I meet Matt at a bar playing "Let's Go Crazy" when I walk in.

"You should see all the white bros at my office." Matt says. "You know that saying, 'white tears.' I'm drowning in them."

"You weren't a fan?"

"I thought I was, but…"

"How's Stasha?"

Matt laughs and flags the bartender. "You really need to call her. She's…" He stops, orders a round, and sits and thinks on his thoughts, "she's not not herself, but oh wow."

"You need some help?"

Matt breathes in, "no. She's so beautiful. I mean, this is what I wanted."

"Good for you."

"How's that girl you were seeing, Denise, Debra?"

"Whoa!" I sip my beer, "that was a long time ago."

"I can't keep up."

"It's not that much to keep up with. That was, like, two years ago."

Matt takes a large swig of beer, "can I tell you something and you don't get offended?"

My spine tenses.

He takes another drink, "I hope our kid's gay. I really do! Every gay person I know is successful, and creative."

"You know that's not how all gay people end up."

"Yeah but we're in Brooklyn. I mean, come on."

"I'll give it to you: things are much different now, but still."

"I'll love my child either way, of course."

"Of course."

"But like, look at Prince."

"Prince was straight!"

"Yeah, but, you know what I mean."

I take a swig of my beer. "I'm not sure that I do."

"This is it for me. The family, the job, the brownstone. The Farinas upstairs are getting old, I could buy them out. This is all I'm gonna do. But a gay kid? Maybe he goes to India, not like to visit, but stays there. Maybe if it's a girl, she'll get into rock, join a band, get famous. I wanna watch my kid go on tour, or walk the red carpet, or a catwalk!"

Matt takes another long swig, feeling the beer in him. "I mean, this person isn't even here yet and I already want so much of the world for them. You know?"

I close my eyes for a beat. "No, Matt. I don't know."

"Well, you can have kids too. There's all sorts of ways."

"It's not about that, Matt." It's my turn to take a long swig of beer. "I'll love my niece or nephew no matter what. But I'll love them for being who they are. I don't care if they're gay or straight or transgender. But I know this life. This particular kind of loneliness. You don't see it, Stasha doesn't see it, Mom and Dad don't see it. But it's there. You think Prince was daring? Tell that to a trans woman in North Carolina right now."

Matt turns his head down to stare into his pint.

"Matt, I know you mean well. I didn't mean to snap at you."

"Oh, I'm used to it now," he laughs.

"You've got all the time in the world to be a father and think and wonder what that means, but you've only got a few months left of being just the husband. Maybe, you should go back home to Stasha."

"You're right. I'll get our drinks."

"I know you will, Wall Street. I'm in mourning."

Matt laughs again. "Dale, are you happy with your life? Are you happy?"

"Most days, Matt. Most days."

May

When my dad calls it's good news.

"They aren't ready to say remission, yet." He says and then he chuckles, "but I almost pried it out of them."

"That's amazing, Daddy."

"Your mother doesn't want me to fly, but I'm coming up to the baby shower. Can't wait to meet my grandson."

"We don't know the gender yet, Daddy."

"There's enough women in the family. Time for a boy."

June

My dad's thinner but his skin looks well. He's still a deep brick, reddish brown when we meet them at the airport. But he walks slow. It takes a while to get the bags from the carousel and fit ourselves into a taxi.

Leah keeps texting me. She wants to bring 49 pebbles to the baby shower, for Pulse. I don't answer her anymore because I told her it's not appropriate. I told her she can't come.

Two of Stasha's sorority friends make a point to tell me they changed their Facebook profile pictures to the Pulse logo. I don't even know what that looks like.

The gender reveal is in the cake. Stasha and Matt make a big deal of it. They had the OB-GYN write a note to the bakery shop, so even they don't know. Stasha looks exactly the same, but with a bowling ball in her stomach. I think she plays up sitting down and standing up, but it'll get real for her later. Stasha and Matt grip the cake knife together and everyone's camera phones start recording. They lift up a pink slice coated in white frosting. Stasha's friends scream.

My dad makes his way up to me, presses a strand of my dreadlocks between his fingers.

"Another girl, Daddy." I say, "what do you think?"

He wipes a tear from my cheek I didn't even realize was there.

"She's gonna be a blessing."

July

Her name is Harriet and she was alive for three days. I move from the hospital waiting room couches to Stasha and Matt's living room. Neither talk to me, or anyone. I keep their phones charged and answer them when they ring. Matt's parents cut their vacation short but Matt doesn't want to see them. Mom and Daddy offer to fly up again but Stasha says no. I haven't really seen her since the day she gave birth. But two weeks after, when Matt has to go back to work, Stasha calls for me from their back bedroom.

She's in bed with a pair of scissors, strips of her weave in her lap.

"What did I do?" Stasha asks.

"Aww, you just cut your hair. We'll get it fixed."

"No, what did I do? What did I do to my baby?"

She collapses into herself. I try to pull her up but she's limp and keeps crying.

"You didn't do anything, Stasha. She was just too good for this world."

"Don't talk to me about my baby!" Stasha yells and pushes my hands off of her.

"I'm trying to help. Tell me what I can do."

"You can't do shit!" She sneers her face at me, "you never do shit, Dale. You spend your whole career doing what? Tweeting for a can of juice? You. Don't. Make. Anything. She could have done anything. She was beautiful. And she was amazing. She could have taken over a room instead of stand against the wall like you."

"Stasha, you're talking a lot." I try to bring her down.

"Stop trying to help me!" Stasha screams, "you can't help me."

"Just tell me what to do!"

"Get the fuck out, you fucking dyke."

August

I sleep with three different women. It's like they can smell the pain on me. And they each try their best, but they can't do what Jameson does. I ask every one into the bathroom with me after I shower, to see if they see the face laid over mine. None of them can. They tell me I'm still drunk, but I know it's there.

"You know Stasha's sorry." Daddy says on the phone, "but she's like your mom. She might not admit it. Doesn't mean it's not there."

Daddy talks about remission in between chemo sessions.

September

My white boss calls me into his office with HR-appointed witnesses from Accounting. They're all white. My boss found an agency that offers multiple social media platforms and a team of fifteen people. They're somehow half the cost of me. My job gets eliminated.

Leah wants to spend the night but I tell her no. She asks about the baby and I realize we haven't spoken in that long.

One night, I get a text from Matt: "Help."

I text back, "Is everything okay? Is Stasha okay?"

"She's OK. But is anyone gonna ask about me?"

"Are you okay?"

"I'm dealing but everything hurts."

"I hurt too. You'll get through this."

"What if I don't?"

October

Matt buys tickets to Beyonce's Formation tour to reunite Stasha and me, but she doesn't show. I put my coat on the extra seat. Beyonce ends with "Halo" in three different types of renditions. She ends with an acapella version and the audience puts their cell phones to flashlight mode. The whole stadium lights up and the dots of white light float against the shadows like dancing stars. Beyonce singing "I can see your halo" sticks with me for weeks.

November

Daddy moves into hospice two days after Trump gets elected President. I fly down, take a shower in my old house and see the face again. It's brighter but the holes over my eyes are darker somehow. I have to strain to see my face through it and the fog on the mirror.

My mother hugs me, "it's okay," she says, "Stasha and Matt are coming down tomorrow."

My father is brown red skin, and bones. He's plugged up to tubes in the hospice bed. Reaching out to open his arms to hug me, the tubing stretches like saliva from an open mouth.

I sit on the bed next to my father. I can feel the bones in his hands wrap around my palms as he tries to hold my hands.

"Your mother," he says. "She's not here?"

"No, Daddy."

"I wanted to tell you, Dale, about your name. I never told you who you're named after."

"It's not your uncle?"

"That's what your mother says," he takes a deep, labored breath. "She doesn't know. Dale was the kind of friend… you don't tell your wife about."

"Daddy?"

"I saw him the first time I laid eyes on you." He wheezes, "you don't look like him. But it's in the eyes."

Daddy coughs and it drags out longer than for a normal person.

"When I married your mother. He didn't come up, but my mother. Her friends said he cried for days.

"He was a good man. All he ever did was take in the world. When it didn't make sense, especially when it didn't make sense."

"No one knew how strong he was, not like I did."

"What happened to Dale, Daddy?"

"He died in the 80s. One of those. I married your mother at 23, never saw Dale again. But then I saw you."

Daddy coughs again, and then says, "you were just a baby, but your eyes held me like his. You make people feel safe, Dale. That's your gift."

"Daddy…"

"This remission ain't coming. Not the way I want it. Tomorrow, Stasha will come but today is for you, Dale."

He grips my hands and his skin feels like paper.

"Since the day you were born, Dale, I loved you like I've never loved anyone else. You hold the world."

We bury Daddy before Thanksgiving.

December

I meet Matt at Penn Station, on his way to Newark to catch a flight to India. He's a mess of tears, crying about Stasha, not knowing where his marriage is. He doesn't want to go, he says, but I know he has to.

We hug and it feels like the first time he's exhaled all day.

"Totally honest, I don't know when I'm coming back," he says.

"You'll come back when you're ready."

"I don't know what that means!" The tears come rushing into his eyes.

"We're never going to be ready. Not for the big things. It's just one step in front of the other."

Matt gives me a hug, and whispers, "I hope you're still my sister when I get back."

I'm still on unemployment, so I have a lot of time for research. I pose as a Journalism major and talk to scientists about my bathroom mirror. They tell me about Scatter Effect. About light refracting around the prisms of steam droplets and condensation on the mirror. An Atmospheric Chemist tells me it's like Aurora Borealis. But none of them can quite explain the face, the black hollow sockets where my eyes should be. Where they are once I make the effort to look through it.

And I can catch the face outside of the bathroom. I see it once in the mirror of a smoky after party with Leah, right before Christmas. I see it in sleet once, near Times Square. All the tourists and Christmas shoppers bend around me running for umbrellas for $5 a pop. But I stare at my reflection in the glass of a skyscraper. The face that pokes out, so obvious, but no one seems to see it.

I close my eyes and accept it. Fuck the science. And fuck ghosts. This is just who I am. I open my eyes and the skull on top of me stares back at me.

Localized Politics

It starts as a small brown stain at the bottom of your paper coffee cup. Everyone else in the campaign office tosses theirs out at the end of the day, but you keep yours. You grip it to feel the numb burn of the coffee on your fingers while you smoke a cigarette in the other hand. You stay until the canvass comes back. Everyone else leaves.

The paper cup gets less stable every day. But you keep using it.

You broke the district up into the 3 large maps that take up the whole wall behind your desk. You don't even live here but the streets feel etched into the palms of your hands now. You breathe in coffee steam, breathe out cigarette smoke. Poll site locations freckle your brain. You used to be someone, two months ago before this campaign, but you have trouble stretching your memory back that far. You don't answer to anything in particular anymore. You just answer every question you know.

Your candidate is beautiful and human. Box braids swirl out from her scalp into a controlled tangle of curls that fall just past her shoulders. She looks everyone in the eye, like politicians are supposed to. But when you talk, you can see that her eyes dance around, crunching numbers.

Some days, in between fundraising calls, local press interviews and senior home visits, when she's got a few minutes of nothing, you see her walk up the district maps like a visitor in a museum.

The campaign gets halfway through the second sweep through the district when the hate mail starts coming in. The first one was a scribbled picture that you almost thought was elementary school art. Until you look closely at it, see the frantic red lines from her neck, chest and groin and realize they're meant to be blood. There's some quick energy around the office, from paid canvassers to volunteers, to see it. To look at real, actual hate mail. You spill your coffee on it. Tell everyone to get back to work.

That's the last day you remember consciously, physically eating food; you couldn't finish your sandwich. One month left til Election Day.

The third sweep through the district is when you see people start to break. The Communications Director screams at a journalist. The volunteers and paid canvassers get jealous of each other and try to horde campaign flyers, clipboards and pens from one another. You're the youngest person on this campaign, watching everyone act like teenagers. The lip of your coffee cup frays at the edge where you put your lips on it. You get stung every sip, the paper doesn't protect you anymore.

The campaign is done with all the white areas—that's what the volunteers complain about. Rude people who won't open their doors, streets that feel unsafe after dark. Your paid canvass is an army, though, they'll go anywhere. The candidate's sister used to come in and knock doors. At first she dressed up but everyone at their homes thought she was a Jehovah's Witness. Then, she started wearing sweat pants or jeans, tied her hair back, wore less make up.

You put her with the paid canvass one shift because everyone thought she was one anyway. And she crushes it, gets higher numbers than the paid crew average. She starts drinking with the canvass after work and starts coming in hungover and sleep deprived. But in the third sweep, she wakes up. During the rap circle practice she gets up, walks to your desk, hands you her clipboard and says, "I need a few days."

Your roommates at home make dinner and leave it for you but you can't eat unless someone places the food in your hands. And you can never finish it. Your throat's gone stiff and swallowing is hard. There's a volunteer who makes phone calls. An old lady. Every few days she comes in with a plate for you and sits with you while you eat. She asks things like whether or not you have a partner, where your parents and family are. And you can only answer back with the campaign.

"My parents live outside the district, but they'd vote for her if they could."

"No dating, no dog. Just me. After the election, I can think about stuff like that."

Your eyes get bloodshot after struggling to swallow. The old lady volunteer offers to bring you a coffee mug from her home, so you can throw the paper cup away. You tell her you're fine, which was not the question she asked.

Your candidate never looks afraid. The opponent dropped a lit-bomb of negative ads in the white neighborhoods. Dog-whistling bullshit about the certain kind of people she used to associate with in college. You try to be as mad as everyone else in the office, until she comes in, smooth, calm, chin up. She studied aerodynamic engineering and calls us all—staff, volunteers, and canvassers—to tell us about drag. The way the air whips chaotically behind a fast moving new object. She tells us we're cutting through the air, we're trying to fly here, and that drag is natural. Some people's response to change is to push back. But if those people ran the world, she says, we'd never be able to fly.

That night you dream that you're so light you start to float. You float out of your own clothes and hover above the sidewalk. You don't have to look around in your dream to know you're in the district. You're always there.

It's hard to do laundry on a campaign but even harder when you're shrinking through your clothes. The campaign office is above an AME church, and once the canvass is gone, the pastor lets you sort through their charity bin for pants that fit you now.

You start prepping for Election Day two weeks out. There's 103 polling locations, that are open from 6am to 9pm. You battle between black and white neighborhoods, who needs more visibility? More staff and volunteers with signs and enthusiasm to get voters into the polls.

You've got voting history saved as a bookmark on your computer so you know where the big volume precincts are and where the small ones are. You do more math modeling than you ever did in college but you were a Sociology major, so go figure. You start scheduling volunteers to staff poll sites but the old lady who feeds you won't go. She says she'll stay with you the whole of Election day.

GOTV is the ramp up, the season finale. The campaign's hit its win number, hypothetically. Now everyone just has to pull the voters out. You have a volunteer team with wheelchair accessible vans. You'll do literally anything to get one of your voters to the ballot.

The bottom of your cup is all black now and wearing down. You have to cup it with one hand underneath and pinch the seams so your coffee doesn't leak. It doesn't always work and your pants and shirt have stains all over them. But they're the only clothes you can wear now. On the bus ride home people think you're homeless.

You don't even bother going home the last two days before the election. You start pouring beer into your paper cup. The night before Election Day, the candidate's sister comes back to the office at 11pm, with pizza and vodka. It's just the two of you. She eats and you drink. Sometimes you try to talk about not-the-election, but you're both so bad at it. She cleans up before she leaves and notices your paper cup. There's reddish brown smudges around the lip—your lip cells are burned and imprinted into it. She picks it up with two pinched fingers and throws it away. You fish it out of the trash after she leaves.

By morning, you've plastered every other wall with giant, real life spreadsheets of polling locations. Where they are, who on the campaign staff is monitoring them, who'll be outside turning out visibility, and at what times, what the last election turnout numbers were like at each precinct, and what part of the win number comes from where. The campaign staff comes in at 5am and you're still scribbling the last bits.

No one says anything. They set their jackets down and stalk up the walls slow, like it's holy. It's not a science, elections; but it's pretty close.

The old lady volunteer comes in at 9am with meatloaf and mashed potatoes on a plate for you, but the phones are ringing non-stop and she knows you need help. Voter protection. You scrawl the cell phone numbers of election attorneys on the little wall space that's left. You tell everyone to answer any phone that rings. They don't stop ringing for 5 hours.

In that time, someone—a volunteer, who knows?—eats your meatloaf plate. Your volunteer tells you she watched the whole thing, but didn't say anything. She says it like a question, like she's unsure. "I didn't say anything?"

For all these months no one, not even you, thought to ask where the candidate's parents were this whole time, until two hours before the polls close and her father, in a sharp black pinstripe suit, walks into the office. He gets pointed out to you and you know who he is before he even says anything, all your candidate's facial features compacted and plastered over his. He smiles and says he knows it's late but he'd like to do anything he could to help, and you freeze.

The sun's been set at this point. There's only a handful of volunteers left, the paid canvass is already on their way to the election night party. For the first time in you life, you stutter. You fish for a call sheet of voters he can call and feel a wet slump in your hand. It's your cup. You've gripped it to death.

One minute after the polls close your cell phone erupts with so many text messages from volunteers that it shuts itself down. You turn it back on and scribble result tabulations. Your volunteer who feeds you sits next to you, and lifts your hand off the leg of your pants so that you can write on paper. No one can read your handwriting, so you get up and kick everyone out of the office. Even your volunteer.

She says no at first and you tell her to get out. She smiles, grips your arms and forgives you. She says softly, "I know. It hurts." And she leaves. You never see her again.

You find your candidate in a back room in her father's arms. They're both waiting like someone's in surgery. You sit down across from them, take a breath, and give the numbers. But that's not what they're hearing. Even she doesn't understand. You have to say it blankly, "you lost."

The sounds starts from inside her chest, but you can still hear it. The groan moves up her throat and out like an explosion. Your candidate is beautiful and human. She cries like her gut is wrenched open for two exact minutes, sniffles and stands up.

Everyone but the volunteer who feeds you is waiting at the after party. Political machine elites are set up at the bar, not talking to anyone. The crowd goes quiet and your candidate concedes the election.

You don't have to pay for any drinks and no one offers you food, just booze. You choke on all of it. Your throat can't even handle liquids anymore. After four drinks you can't stand up. Volunteers shuffle you into a car, and drive out of the district to take you home. You don't know where you are at first, stepping into your apartment. Your roommates are up waiting for the news, with cake and a big banner that says "Congratulations!" But they see it on your face the second you walk in. They don't offer you cake.

You fold yourself into bed. Hug what's left of your belly. You breathe out acid reflux now. Your mouth hangs open like the exhaust pipe of a car.

I Want You

That first year, the clinic told me to pick a time, an easy time that I won't forget, and take the pills then. Every day like that, for the rest of my life. HIV's really good for clearing out your schedule, especially that first year. Guys don't call, or they don't know and then they find out, and then they don't call. My mother called, almost four times a day.

"Did you take your meds?" She'd ask.

"Yes, Mom."

"Maybe you should take one again. Just in case."

"Mom, it doesn't work like that."

"I know." She breathed long into the phone receiver, "maybe you should, anyway."

Over time, retroviral medication tightens facial muscles. I get away with it because I'm Asian. My eyes already look tied at the ends. The meds smooth my forehead lines and, I swear to God, stunt what little facial hair growth I had down to a slow crawl. Today, I look younger than I did when I contracted. It's a damned shame.

I used to take my pills at night, right before bed. Not like there was much else to do in my bed anyway. Right around eleven I'd throw down the white-and-brown capsules, chug some water and drift off. I used to dream crazy adventures: flying, theme park rides, vampires with cheekbones sharp enough to cut you. Now I dream about holding hands with a guy who likes me. I dream about eating ice cream with someone. The sun beats down on us and it's a rush to finish our cups before the whole thing melts. My dreams are fucking e-Harmony commercials.

I've been positive for five years. They make iPhone apps for it now. Eleven o'clock and my phone would buzz. I picked the Uncle Sam icon and he shakes his big index finger at me.

"I want you! ... to take your pills!"

It seemed funny at the time.

A Thursday after work I'm with my co-worker, Wendy, who is single, turning thirty, and has never been to a gay bar. I can't talk my way out of it and now we're screaming at each other over the thudding bass. She's getting jostled by gym-bunny cliques and I'm getting groped a couple of times by drunk twink kids. A skinny Asian is like Pez candy for them.

"Vodka!" I scream to the bartender for the third time.

Wendy's loose after two vodka tonics and she sets me up at a standing table on the outside patio so she can play matchmaker for me. My phone buzzes in the middle of some investment banker telling me about his trip to Fiji. It's supposed to win me over, that he's "okay with the rice." When I flip my phone, Uncle Sam's staring back at me. I excuse myself to go to the bathroom.

I shuffle through my messenger bag twice before I realize that since I wasn't planning on coming out tonight my pills are at home, next to my toothpaste and an empty cup for water.

"Wendy, I gotta go home."

"No!" She's past loose and into full-on drunk.

"Do you need a ride?" Asks the investment banker, "Or I can call a cab?"

"No, stay here!" Wendy says, tugging on my shirt and then leaning her weight on it. She almost pops a button and the banker takes an eye-shot at my chest.

"Let me give you a ride." He says, "You might need help with her."

"I wanna stay!" Wendy huffs. She leans back to cross her arms over her chest but over does it and knocks a group of drinks off the table behind her. Bitchy queens narrow their eyes at her.

"Come on." Says the banker.

In five years I've never not taken my pill on time. Not that I don't think about it. I was the kind of kid who'd do exactly what I was told not to, just to see if the world would really end like every adult made it out to be. Go figure.

We prop Wendy in the back seat of the banker's black sedan and then I clip myself into the shot-gun seat. Uncle Sam wants me again, buzzing loud.

The banker starts the car, "that's not a an ex-boyfriend, is it?"

"Not entirely." I feed Uncle Sam a button so he'll shut up and then tell the banker to head south, toward my apartment. Wendy obliterates some pop song lyrics for a verse and a chorus, then falls asleep.

The banker says, "I'm glad I met you tonight," and I nod. It's 11:13.

"Do you go out often?" He says. "I don't. Not usually."

"Me neither." My right leg starts jack-hammering and I stare at the clock on the dash board. The banker notices and takes his free hand to my knee to settle me and it's the first time a man's actually touched me in years. I can feel the weight and heat from his hand and for a second I can almost remember what it's like to be with a man. When I glance at him, his face is blushed red. The bankers' lips creep a tight smile and he parts them, about to say something, when Wendy's belch from the backseat turns into projectile vomit. I get splashed on the back of my neck and it trickles down my back, between me and the car seat. Wendy starts to cry.

We pull over into a gas station. It's 11:17, Uncle Sam buzzes again and Wendy's into a full wail. The banker rushes to get paper towels and I peel myself out of the seat to get away from the smell. Night air chills my wet shirt and I'm shivering. He comes to me with a towel first, rubs my neck and pats down my back.

25

"Look—" I start.

"No, no. It's okay. These things happen."

It's 11:20. I can't catch my breath. My stomach feels bottomed out and I'm dizzy. This isn't a med reaction. This is what happened five years ago in the clinic, what happened two months later when I told my mom.

My phone buzzes, "I want you!"

I bawled when they told me. Saliva streams stretched from my top teeth to my bottom ones. My chest jerked and heaved. The clinic lady didn't give me any tissue or wide eyes. She sighed, checked her watch, let me cry for two more minutes and then screamed at me.

"Hey!" That shut me up, "I don't feel sorry for you. Billion dollars go into billboards and campaigns and MTV telling you to wrap it up, and what? You didn't notice?"

I steadied out my breathing and she kept going, "No one cares that you slipped up. That doesn't matter anymore. The only thing that matters is what you do now. And this crying, this self-pity thing, it will kill you."

My chest ticked and sent out a charge all the way to my fingers and toes, then it died. I used to feel that when a man was straddled on top of me. When he'd rub his hands up my stomach, over my chest, tongue-kiss me and then pull back to glare bedroom eyes at me.

It's 11:25 and I'm gone before I even realize it. The gas station's two blocks behind me and my apartment's not far, just over a small hill up the way. Headlights clip past the sides of my face and a car honks. The banker's sedan rolls up to my side. Wendy's asleep in the front seat and the banker rolls down his window.

"You don't have to be embarrassed. It's all cleaned up now. Brand new."

I don't say anything back to him.

"I lied," he says. "I go to that bar four nights a week."

Uncle Sam in my pocket wants me again.

"It's the same shit all the time. The same faces."

11:27. Uncle Sam beeps.

"The boyfriend again, huh?" Says the banker, "let me just take you and 'fun-times' here home, okay. I'm not gonna meddle."

"I don't have a boyfriend. It's an app." I can't control my mouth, it goes on without me, "Reminding me to take my meds."

"What kind of meds?"

"Viral. I'm poz."

The banker chuckles, "Whew, okay. You almost scared me there."

"What?"

"Meds, you know? I thought you were crazy. Like, clinically."

"I am clinical. I'm positive."

"Okay. And I'm not. Get in the car."

He settles on my couch while I go chug my pills. I tilt my head back, feeling them slide down. I usually don't enjoy the pills, this time I do. Then I turn off my cell phone. The banker's sitting on my recliner, flipping through cable channels.

"Why do you take your meds at night? Couldn't you take them during the day?"

I shrug.

He fidgets the remote between his hands. Cute, like a nervous teenager and says, "During the day maybe you know, someone could remind you?"

"Thanks," I say. "For tonight. It's getting late."

"Yeah, okay, I'll get out of your hair." He stands up and I walk him toward the door. He stops his hand at the door knob and says, "I want you."

"Huh?"

"No," he says, "that came out wrong. I want… to go on a date with you. You know, sometime, if you have the time."

"I have time." I say and he kisses me, right then just on the cheek. His lips linger there for a second and pull back. His face is bright red again, like in the car earlier. But this time Wendy's not interrupting us. I watch the red in his cheeks fade, watch his mouth relax so that his temples bulge just a bit and recede. His eyebrow curls, like he's asking me a question, and I feel it. That tight tick in my chest that shoots electricity all the way to the edges of my pinkie fingers. The spark that seized my fingers dialing my mother's number five years ago to tell her.

It's the feeling that something owns you, that something can pull your body from the inside in ways no one can see on the outside. The banker guy, eyebrow creased, shoulders slacked, not embarrassed anymore, splits a slight smile from the corner of his lips and that tick comes again, sucking the air right out of me. He finally says goodnight and walks out, but I stand there dumbstruck in the doorway. I stand there for I don't know how long.

Money Men

The television's always on when I get into the room and usually it's the news. These guys are convention-goers and they need to know the latest. Big money guys, they don't even bother to turn off the TV. They just mute it, lay down on the bed, fold their hands behind their heads and watch me unzip my dress. The big money guys won't move an inch for their own orgasm; that's why they're outsourcing it. One guy twists me around so he can watch my back curve and I watch CNN. That's when I first hear about Tunisia.

The anchor guy's muted mouth moves around as headlines scroll underneath about self-immolation, uprisings and dictators. Then they show a clip of the street footage. It looks like LA cleared out for a movie shoot. Out of the corner come the people. They wear bandanas around their faces, for the tear gas, and hold their Arabic protest signs like shields. The camera pans onto one man. His face sneers out in anger screaming something in Arabic but I can tell he's handsome. I lean closer to the TV screen and that somehow does it for the money man underneath me. I make $500.

Mornings, I work the checkout aisle at the grocery store near my condo. The only current events people talk about are store gossip. Who's fucking who in the meat department, and then giggles about "meat department." They can't point out Tunisia on a map. I tell Alma, at the next register, it's the place where they filmed the desert stuff in those Star Wars movies.

"Isn't it funny, because the originals were all about uprising." I tell her.

"Sandra, when you start talking geek I don't even follow you."

I've always lived in the suburbs. My parents own some prefab deal with more space than two people ever need. There's rooms they haven't set foot in since '99. They think that makes them rich. My condo is nestled in Buckhead and, at night, the Atlanta skyline glows, casting kaleidoscope glimmers through the windows and onto my walls. The view puts me into the bank for over a million dollars.

I pick up the New York Times after shopping for dresses on 10th Street and read about Tunisia while I eat lunch at the Indian sidewalk cafe. Self-immolation is setting yourself on fire. People do that. This college grad in Sidi Bouzid got fined for selling produce on the side of the road and couldn't afford the ticket. He made what's equivalent to $7 a day.

Back at home, I take pictures of myself in the new dresses for my Craigslist ads and end up Google searching pictures of Tunisian protestors. I would have pictured them darker-skinned in robes or some kind of garb, but they look like they could be anyone going through my check out lane. Well, if you minus the screaming, the fire, the signs, the tear gas and the police beating them. I do, I look at these men and wipe away all the struggle. I try to look into their eyes.

My men are not classically attractive. Most have belly guts and splotchy skin. Most haven't had hair for some years now. But they're not hideous. They usually have wedding rings so I figure someone loves them, and that helps. I watch their eyes beam up at me when I'm on top and, for a few minutes, I could swear they're models: young, robust and oozing out sex. Sometimes I can wipe away the money and the hotel smell.

One man flips me on the bed, stomach-down and comes in from behind. He doesn't even bother to mute the TV in front of me. This is how I hear about Egypt. They show Tahrir Square and it looks like a music festival, minus the military tanks, gunfire and triage bandages. I try to read the scroll but the man's thrusting bobs my head up and down. I just watch the crowd blur and refocus.

"You like that? Huh?" From the money man.

"Yes," I say.

More customers buy tabloids than newspapers which drives me to ask some of them, "have you heard what's happening in Egypt?" I get back blank stares until someone finally bites. He's a caramel skinned young man, early twenties, with sharp black ringlets of curly hair. He looks too dark-skinned but just young enough to light himself on fire. He tells me about a rally tomorrow, downtown in front of the capital building. But that's too close for a working girl; I don't want to see clients in the sunlight.

I catch it on mute later on in the night. The brown boy's saying something to a reporter. I recognize that his white shirt, red jacket and black shorts are the colors on Egypt's flag.

* * *

I buy the darkest spray-on tan I can find and get some fabric from a Moroccan boutique where they teach me how to wrap myself up in hijabs. Fake-browned and veiled, I put out an ad on Craigslist. The ad says something about being new to America and being scared, "given what's happening." I get a money man in two minutes. He'll pay $3,000. He's got a room at the Hilton near the Civic Center. The TV's off when I get there; he's got papers spread out over his desk, table and chairs. His laptop's open to a Power Point with pie-graphs.

He has me undress slow and once I'm naked he throws me onto the bed. He bites down hard on my neck and ears. I try to reach for the remote on the night stand but he grabs my hands and presses them into a pillow while he unzips and slips down his pants. Then he clamps both hands hard on my neck and digs inside me.

"Say something in Arabic, bitch!"

He pushes my neck down into the mattress and my lungs seize for air. I gag on my own tongue but somehow pull from what I've overheard this whole time.

"Tahrir, horreyah," I say. Arabic for Liberation, Freedom.

My blood's on the mattress when he's done. Red on white bed sheets, next to his black dress slacks. He tries to say something about I'm sorry but I grab the cash and my clothes. I get dressed in the elevator.

For days, I stay at home, plugged into Al Jazeera English. Instead of online shopping I read blogs. I set up a Twitter account to get live updates. The caramel brown boy comes through my line again, buying beer, and slips me a flier for another rally. Mubarak resigns later that day.

I get to the rally at 5:30, wearing sunglasses with my hair tied up in a bandana. I try to be invisible on the outer rim of the crowd, but strangers keep approaching. They pass out middle eastern candies, tea, cookies and hugs. Their squeezes vibrate my spine and I lie about the breeze making me cold. This just gets me more tea.

The crowd decides to march in celebration and I'm thrusted a sign that says "Revolution in the Middle East." I find a group of young girls in hijabs and follow them. They take turns screaming chants and passing water bottles so they don't lose their voice. All the girls are crying, tears collecting in the fabric under their chin.

Watching them, I decide that I'm done placing money-man ads.

* * *

I first hear about Libya in my condo. With full coverage news, the Al Jazeera English streaming feed and Twitter, I try to wipe away my Ramen noodle dinner, my swelling stack of bills, and my part-time grocery store job for $9 an hour. But it won't work. I pull up Craigslist.

I find a money man at the Marriott, the standard 500 dollars. He's got thick jowls that blend into a double chin and he smells like ham. On top, I force my pelvis down hard on him and then dig my nails into the skin of his man-breasts. He tries to touch my hair but I slap his hand away every time. His cum-moans are sing-song. He pays me double.

I tell the next money man that I need the TV on, full blast. I grip the skin just over his cheekbones with my teeth and sink in. The US news spreads bullshit about the Muslim Brotherhood that Al Jazeera, Twitter and Mother Jones refute. Obama's lip service about peaceful transitions boils me up so fast I slug another money man across the face without even realizing it. He offers me extra to fall asleep in bed with him.

I first hear about Wisconsin while biting down hard on a money man's nipples. I'm drawing blood, he's moaning. When Wolf Blitzer says "America" and "uprising" in the same sentence I let my teeth up and dart my eyes toward the TV.

"Don't stop." The money man says.

An embed correspondent is in the thick of the protest, with thousands behind him in winter coats shaking their signs toward the camera. The money man makes a grab for my breast and I slap his hand.

The movement: it's come across the ocean. I swat my hand one more time at the money man and he catches it.

"I'm paying you—" He tries, but the TV volume fills my ears with solidarity chants and the loud tide roar of hundreds of voices meeting up as one and I lunge my free hand at the money man's throat.

"You bitch!" He chokes. I shift my legs up quickly over the mound of his stomach and punch him with all I've got. I growl and then grab his face into mine for a rough, lip-biting kiss. American protestors cheer.

"'You like that? Huh?'" I say, and then I grab what hair he has left to crane him up again for another punch. He coughs on his blood while I shove a knee just under his rib cage. Adrenaline snaps in him too and the girth of him pins me down. He holds me there, blood dripping from his nose onto my breasts. His face starts to look like all the other money men: Ben Ali, Mubarak, Al Khalifa, Qaddafi, Walker.

"'Say something in Arabic, bitch!'" I scream and something about that makes him cry. Blood, snot, and tears, it all falls down on me. I sneer and try to pry my way out from him, but the money man's big hands keep me down. Then he falls on me, sobbing, and still won't let me go. We lay there for two hours, every few minutes I try to escape and every few minutes he hugs me tighter. I growl and he whimpers. Once he's asleep I wiggle out from under him and grab his wallet, then his pants, then his suitcase and laptop. I toss his clothes off an I-75 overpass and leave his suitcase and laptop with a bunch of squatters behind a Wal-mart parking lot.

* * *

At work, people talk about Wisconsin now. It's finally gossip-worthy because it's happening in America. I don't waste my breath to tell them about the thousands dead, the price of food, or the young men setting themselves on fire. I keep back all the money men faces, the spent condoms, and business suits and I wait for that curly-haired caramel skin boy to come back to my line, for him to pass me another flier. I'll go with him, to Madison, to Syria. I picture us bandana'ed and arm-locked; he'll have a protest sign for our shield and I'll have the kerosene. I'll be ready to light our lives up flames.

Death and Taxes

"I told her my friend died a few days ago in Rwanda." He says, slipping his leg over mine and then rubbing his heel up and down my calf.

"My sister's a hundred words a minute," he says. "She's going off about political turmoil, globalization and child-soldiers. And then she gets quiet. She says, 'Do you know how?' I'm like, 'how what?'"

He slides his shoulder up toward me on a pillow and leans up, his lips close to my lips, "she makes that sound, that slit-your-throat sound. She can't even say the words."

"Can you?" I ask him. His eyes run down my neck and chest and then up again.

"Death. Dying. Dead." And then he laughs, "I'm not afraid of it."

I smile at him, "yeah, I'm not either."

"Easy for *you* to say, old man" he says. I roll on my back and kick his leg off of me.

"Get off it," I tell him.

"Off what?" He straddles me, digging his knees in the mattress on either side of my hips.

"You think you'll live forever," I say.

"I think I'll out-survive you," he says.

My hips feel his pulse from his thighs.

"So what'd your sister say?"

"Well, I told her he got T-boned in an intersection and she said, 'that's how most Americans go.'"

After Mom died Dad couldn't live in the house alone. Me and Charlie stopped by that day and Dad was sitting at the kitchen table, waiting for the coffee to brew. He didn't look at us, just said, "the beds are made up in your old rooms." Charlie left two days after the funeral. My dad waved good-bye to her with one hand and clenched mine in the other.

Every night I could hear Dad waking up to the sound of his own cough. The floorboards groaned as he fetched water. I would stare at the ceiling and count his wheezing exhales. After about five, I heard him crying. I knew he was dreaming about her.

He cranes down to nuzzle his cheek against my chest and I feel the flecks of his stubble.

"I don't think we go anywhere after we die," he says.

"No?"

"No, do you?"

I sigh and lift my eyes toward the ceiling, "I have no idea."

"It's gotta be all bullshit. Heaven and Hell."

"It has to be?"

He nods his facial hair against me. "Yeah," he says.

"I don't want to be cremated." I tell him. He doesn't move. "When I die, I don't want to be cremated. Everyone says that, 'Just cremate me. I don't want to be remembered in a casket.' But I do. I want people to say goodbye to my face."

He turns his head so that his chin's on me, just above my nipple.

He says, "You think I'll still be in the picture when you die? You think we'll make it that long?" His lips curl in the corners.

"No," I say, "I just tell everyone that. Just in case I drop dead."

"I don't believe you." He studies my face until his lips part, just a little.

"What?" I ask. I feel my armpits sweat. "I don't believe in Heaven, either."

My rum kept going missing. I thought I was blacking out. I counted back the days, tried to reconstruct the ice, the liquor and the Diet Coke. Then I found Dad's vomit-soaked sheets on top of the washing machine. He wouldn't speak anymore, just drank spiked coffee and soda. I did the housekeeping, the shopping. I kept the drunk ghost alive.

Every few days I'd hear my father hit the floor like tumbling rocks. I told him he'd break the other hip that way. One time, I bent over to heave him up, and when all his old weight rested on my left side I felt his wet warmth spread from his pajama pants to my jeans. Dad let out a drunk chuckle.

Charlie said I stay with him because I want to, because I have bad taste in men.

"That's what Mom left us with," she said.

"In high school, my buddy, Keith, wrote this essay about government, you know, protecting the people, all that," I say. "It got in some contest and won. He was supposed to fly to DC, meet the President, photo-ops."

"Supposed to?" He says.

"We lived in this bad neighborhood growing up. He was two weeks away from meeting the President. Crossfire. Some gang thing."

"Some gang thing?"

"Closed casket."

My dad took to calling me "faggot." Not as a name or a pronoun, just when the silence stretched between us and we were alone. It was like fighting words. Dad was trying to get under my skin. He'd say faggot when I cooked dinner, when the audio on the TV was low enough, when I had to help him wipe his own ass.

I never took the bait though, just treated him like he had Tourette's.

He settles into the groove of my arm and pokes his finger at my nipple. Then he says, "I used to want to die. Not like suicidal, or anything. But when I was a kid, I was obsessed with it."

"Suicide?"

"No, whether something happens after. Like, I used to wonder about reincarnation and if I slit my wrists, would I wake up as a new born baby in China?"

I don't respond, just breathe in deep.

"And, then, like last year, I got real drunk, on a date with some loser. And—this is so stupid, don't judge me—but I walked into a wall. I fell down on the floor. And I swear, for a second, I had a choice in it. If I wanted to stay awake, I could have. But I let go. I remember thinking, 'fuck it.' and drifting off. It felt like peace, like this big warm blanket coming over me."

"That wall right there is pretty sturdy," I say.

"Fuck you," he says, finger still on my nipple. "It was just one moment. Most times, I'm trying everything to be alive, live life and, that one time, I just gave up."

"How'd it feel?"

"Concussions feel great. You sleep so hard."

I left the house twice in one week and both times when I came back my father was on the floor. He felt like sandbags tied together when I'd try to lift him, onto the nearby chair or the couch. Dad was really good at being dead weight.

"What would you have done if I didn't come back, Dad? You would have lived there on the floor?"

He pulled his head up by the neck to look at me, and said, "I live here."

"Yeah, technically, I guess."

Then I went to the kitchen to put some coffee on. He yelled faggot from the living room. I walked back and met him in the eyes.

"Do you even know what you're saying?" I asked, "sometimes I wonder if you had a stroke while I wasn't looking. Dad, that's how drunk you are."

"I don't think you're obsessed with it," I say to him. "I think you're drawn to it."

"No, I'm not a Scorpio."

"Who said you were? But you know, there's some people who could skate close to the edge of it and come back still themselves."

"Like those stories about sky drivers who hit the ground but get up and walk away?"

"Like I watched my father die downstairs."

"The fuck?!"

"No, he was old, and drunk and widowed." I lie and say this happened a while ago. "We were watching TV, well I was, he was struggling to put rum to his mouth. And he drops the cup, pushes it off his lap. I thought it'd break but he didn't have enough muscle in him."

This young guy stops with my nipple and brings his eyes up to mine.

I keep going, "neither one of us tried to move. I was still eating my dinner. And he slumps. He had that death rattle, but it sounds like a cough that never gets hard enough air. Like the life just leaks out of him."

"I'm so sorry," he says. "That's a lot to deal with."

"I finished eating."

"Really?"

"Yeah, my mom would have wanted me to."

"She was that much of a stickler for family dinner?"

"No, she just hated him. And it took me that long to see it, but, I hated him too."

Hope It Felt Good

This is what happens when your man fucks Celia Washington. First, you know already. There's a twitch in your pinky finger when he kisses you, when he pulls back from your face with his eyes still closed, and when his wipe-on smile reminds you of those dumbass erectile dysfunction commercials with the idiot man who never talked but always grinned at any and every one, like a hard-on dick is the only thing that keeps the world turning.

Then he starts taking up racquetball, which you find out later is cheat-code for Celia Washington. You tell him you'd like to play racquetball too sometime but he says it's a guy thing, and makes a whole monument for it. New shoes, expensive boxers. He whistles in the shower and then whistles that same tune fetching his shit into his brand new duffel bag. And you know, you know but you don't know, and your mind doesn't like getting clouded with all that and work's getting stressful anyway. You know, but you leave it alone.

Then you see Celia Washington at the grocery store and she's dolled up in a half-see-through top, dangly earrings and pin-striped black slacks—business appropriate for skanks—and she winks at you and laughs to herself. And this isn't high school anymore and you make more money than she does and your husband's playing racquetball to get into shape but you still want to snatch handfuls of her hair and rip them free from her scalp but you don't because this isn't high school anymore and you do make more money than her and your husband is getting in shape with racquetball and you figure you've already won this one.

Then your husband goes on the road for work when you never thought managing a call center required out of town trips. He leaves his gym bag home once and you decide to wash the stench of sweaty man-boxers out of it only to find the bag doesn't stink at all.

When your husband finally tells you he's fucking Celia Washington, your ears fill with room-tone. It's not quite sound, but it's definitely not noise. And it's the first time in six months he's not grinning like a two-dollar-idiot, and your vision crisps so sharp you can see every scraggly outline of lint on his jacket, and his breath feels like ten thousand wet pellets splashing your face as he says I'm sorry, I'm so so sorry. And you remember that shit-eating tune he'd whistled this whole time, and you remember the rumor Celia Washington spread about your pubic hair in high school, and you remember what your husband's dick felt like when he got it hard, except now it's fuzzy because it's a memory and because he's not getting it hard for you anymore, and you remember you're holding onto a glass pitcher of iced tea.

Your husband probably has a concussion now, stammering out of the kitchen and bumping his shoulders against every door frame but you're irrationally worried about tiny glass shards stuck in the carpet. This is what happens when your man fucks Celia Washington. You can't blink anymore, you're vision never blurs again and high pitched noises bother you. And bright lights, and white teeth, and the hamster that runs on the spinning wheel in your brain that turns so you can think runs at light speed all the time now. And you and your husband go to marriage counseling and you stare at the paisley print patterns of the psychotherapist's ties and it makes you dizzy. And you find Celia Washington's address online and drive the ten minutes out of the way after work to creep by her apartment and you tell your husband this and you tell the therapist this and they both say to stop it but you can't.

This is what happens when your man fucks Celia Washington: he says he's sorry all day and every day and in bed he nuzzles up to you so he can cry into your breasts and feel your heartbeat except your skin's too damned hot and you evaporate his shit-tears, and he wonders if you're running a fever but you don't because you've never felt stronger your whole life and you dream about pounding Celia Washington's head into the sidewalk curb outside her apartment and in your dream you take bites out of her cheeks and chew and swallow with her blood slipping down your neck and your husband standing next you with that plastered erectile dysfunction grin.

Your husband and the therapist agree it's time to start trying for kids again but you haven't menstruated since your man fucked Celia Washington and the gynos around town don't know why because you're still decades from menopause and your husband hasn't not cried for almost a year now.

"Your touch burns me," your husband says, trying to navigate his dick inside you. One shove against his shoulder throws your husband off of you. You realize your feet can hang off the bed now and that they never used to.

Your co-workers haven't eaten lunch with you since your husband was fucking Celia Washington because you don't talk anymore, and because you can swallow anything after one chew, and because you're never not hungry and you take food off their plates without asking, but also because the curls in your hair have straightened and your cheekbones have filled out and your skin glimmers after two minutes in the sunshine and you attract too much attention at restaurants.

At home you're growing out of your clothes as faster than a toddler does and even your baggy bedtime shirts hang above your waistline. Your husband thinks you're beautiful now but he should have thought about that more before he started fucking Celia Washington. It's too late now but he's too afraid to leave you or do anything with another woman because you're taller than he is and you're stronger than he is and you both know you could burn him just by holding onto him, that the furnace inside you can more than castrate him, and you haven't seen him smile for two years now and that makes you smile, and he says he's sorry so many times every day you both have forgotten what your voice sounds like.

And then there's the business of that little bitch, Celia Washington.

You go through her garbage at night, not to dig up dirt or steal some secret from her. You go through her garbage at night so you can train your nose on the smell of her, so that you can tell the difference between a plastic spoon Celia Washington held in her hand once last week and a plastic spoon she put in her mouth once last week. And you catch whiffs of Celia Washington all over town, and you know when she goes to the nail salon and how often she restocks her groceries, and Celia Washington knows you're doing this too because everyone in town can see you doing it. Everyone can see you stretching the seams of anything you're wearing and flaring your nostrils on street intersections so you can catch the scent of her, and everyone can see steam coming off of you on those crisp late autumn days when the temperature just drops and you're more than two feet taller than the high school basketball team now and moonlight is the only kind of light left that doesn't hurt your eyes and everyone knows not to look you in the eyes, or bump past you without pleading for forgiveness, or not cut you off in traffic or stand in front of you at the grocery store checkout lane, because everyone knows now what happens when your man fucks Celia Washington.

Super Rush

I buy a bottle of poppers as an aspirational purchase, like keeping a condom in your wallet. You know, just in case. The brand I get is called Super Rush, it's on the shelf with other double entendres like Surge, Stroke, and Heat. My bottle is about the size of two short Bic lighters, and summer is my travel season. I can pack it anywhere.

I spend most of my time on the road getting drunk in hotel bars and fantasizing about some sexy stranger picking me up. It used to be that these sexy strangers were all chiseled, slightly Greek-looking, and muscular, but I've seen too hotel bars near America's airports. So even in my fantasies I started settling.

The guy in the black pin-striped blazer with the deep red tie but eagle-hooked nose and bifocals, he could do. Or maybe the cute and chubby flight attendant who gave me an extra bag of pretzels and a smile. He could do, too. Of course I don't ever speak to any of these guys. The few times I've tried all the words float out of my head like pictures of the jetstream and then disperse.

I'm in Phoenix for a trade show, at some gay bar an $8 dollar Uber ride from downtown, and I suddenly think, "fuck it." I go back to my hotel room, grab the Super Rush from the front pouch of my carry-on and Google gay bathhouses. Phoenix has two, both on the edge of town in different directions. I know if I stop moving and start thinking I'll chicken out, so I pick the one named Club Phoenix because that's easy to remember.

It's Saturday night and there's a line out the door. Good sign, I guess? This is only the second time I've done this and the first was years ago. I was drunk and stupid and had beer goggles for some guy whose name and face I can't remember anymore.

I get a standard room, $35 for 8 hours, and undress in there. The full length mirror next to the bed doesn't do me any favors. When I exhale and slouch a little, my stomach plugs out in front me like a watermelon. If I suck in I look like I might have muscles. But holding that in the whole night is gonna be a challenge.

I see myself naked all the time, but this is the first time in a while I've actually studied myself. My chest hair is getting longer and wiry. My Treasure Trail used to fall flat, like a sparse brown forest. Now the hairs are thicker and starting to bend. And then there's the obvious—I'm a grower not a show-er. Standing there, I look like Michelangelo's David gave up.

I wrap a towel around and I look better. Grab the room key and the poppers. Struggle awkwardly with how to hold everything. I whisper, "fuck it," to myself a few times before stepping out. These past few years of playing it safe, hoping and dreaming but ending my nights watching porn. I need a break.

I head to the group showers first. They're tucked away, past an open room with gym equipment. No one's working out; it's past midnight. There's one other guy showering, young. The water rolls over the smooth mounds of his ass, a good start to the night. I try not to be pervy so I take the showerhead one over from him. The hot water blasts and even in the dim lighting I see the pale skin of my shoulders getting beat pink. I catch the young guy out of the corner of my eye. He's turning around to face the entrance and fondle himself. We lock eyes and he gives me a smile that I feel in my groin.

Water in my mouth catches me off guard and I cough a little. Just enough to call attention to the fact that I was staring at him with my whole mouth open. He turns full frontal toward me, says hi, and that's when we both see it.

Even from a few feet away I can make out the red devil tattoo with the snaky tail coiled underneath, just over the heart. He sees it too, the same tattoo on me albeit a little covered in coarser hair. The young guy steps out of his shower and walks toward me. I step back to share the shower stream and he puts his hand on my devil tattoo and my hand on his. And then he looks into my eyes like a laser beam scanning for signs of life.

I know he's me, but I really know he's me when he furrows his brow a little, the same way I do.

"The fuck?" he says to me like a question he wants answered. And somewhere inside of me, under the layer of beer fat and the nine month dry spell of not having sex, a spark jolts my arms. I grab him by the back of his/my neck and pull his/my face into mine. I know how I kiss. I keep my mouth closed at first to gauge the other guy, to see who's gonna step up first. I know this, so I take charge. I push my tongue against his teeth. My hands slide down his back muscles and I can feel him/me relax and breathe deep as he opens his mouth for my tongue.

When I touch him, I can feel it on myself like a memory. We stop kissing and my hands go everywhere on him and his chest expands and contracts, breathing deep.

I say, "My room?" And he nods slow.

We're both confused, bumping into ourselves, walking back to my room. I fumble the keys, drop them, but he's there to catch them before they've hit the ground. We already know everything about each other/ourselves. When we get in the room, he sits next to me on the bed and smooths his finger over one of my eye brows, then does the same to himself.

"I," he says and then trails off. It's my voice but like hearing it on playback. "I don't know how..."

He answers himself by shifting over to sit on my lap, cupping my face in his hands and kissing me. I, we, are both hard, pushing against myselves.

I get it out when our lips aren't touching, "I'm 35. You're?"

"19," he says.

He grips my dick and positions it to go in. My brain ripples, sliding through his/my internal folds. He tenses up, for just a second, but we're pretty good at bottoming. I ease into myself and he leans back against my arms. Our tattoos are mirror-swapped on us.

After, we lay face-to-face on the twin cot. It's hard to manage, but we know how to compensate for each other. He fingers my nipple while I run my fingers through his hair. My hair's starting to thin towards the back, but his is still full.

"So…" he says and laughs to himself before he keeps going, "I guess I've got that age-old self-esteem question down."

"Huh?"

"'Do you love yourself?' Okay, so it's actually a couple of different kinds of questions, wrapped up in one."

I can't help but smile at myself.

"The first is just point-blank. Gut-level, no thought, just straight reaction. 'Do you love yourself?'"

I take his hand and pool my fingers around his. I can't stop smiling, "well, yeah, that one. It's pretty obvious. What are the other questions?"

"You don't know? Shouldn't you know?"

I shoot back, "shouldn't you be in Florida right now?"

He sighs and searches the room, considering it for the first time. It's like I already know what he'll do. And whenever I move, he's in sync with me.

"Um, what are these?" He says, finding my poppers.

"I don't know," I shrug, "I thought it'd be fun to try."

"Aren't these a drug?"

"You think that. Lots of people think that but they're actually not. The EU just—"

"Nope! If you tell me anything, it better be lottery numbers."

We sit in the jacuzzi with a rotation of guys who come in, make out and then leave together. I sit next to me and he puts his legs on my lap. I get the twenty questions from not quite twenty year old me. I work in sales, I hate it. But I do get to travel. We graduate college on time, but just barely.

"Tell me about boyfriends."

I shrug, "I'm not sure there's much to tell."

"Damn. I knew it."

"Knew what?"

"We think love is some great big ideal, but it's not like Mom and Dad ever had it."

I used to speak with more affect when I was younger, like I was a bad sitcom actor on a television show. I forgot this.

He says, "shit. Someone breaks our heart, don't they?"

"No."

"Don't lie… to yourself."

We both laugh under our breath at that. He splashes a bit of water at me.

"I just want to know that I'm gonna be happy, you know?"

"No." I say, "you want to know if you're gonna get a boyfriend and fall in love."

"Exactly! Aren't those the same thing?" I can hear the sarcasm in myself.

I see myself next in a bathhouse in Washington DC. I'm in the sauna, watching myself get fingered by a bearish middle eastern man. I see me smile at me, nod for me to come over. But I don't move. I take a minute to watch myself in action, bent over. I squint through the dim lighting of the sauna to see what my younger face does when a finger goes deep in me.

Eventually he pulls the man's hand out of him and walks up to me. He plants a warm, long kiss on me, the kind that makes your brain feel like it's rotating sideways. He knows all the little tics to keep my mind in the moment, how to place my hands where I really actually want them to go. He knows when to stop moving my hands so I can find "new" spots on me. We both like the neck, and when he goes in for mine the sauna bevels around us like we're the point of gravity.

We end up in the Middle Eastern man's room, taking turns on myself. I brought my poppers, still unused, and 19 me is the one who rips the plastic, opens it and takes a big sniff while the Middle Eastern man is inside of him.

I remember the head-haze as soon as it starts to take hold in him. The static energy in the air charges and sparks on both our skin. I want to kiss me, but he pushes me by my love-handle until I end up in the Middle Eastern man's mouth. When I get close to cumming, I can feel it. I cum at the same time.

The first time that happened was with a boy in college, and it felt like an accident. He got close and out of nowhere so was I. I thought it meant something, between the two of us, but he stopped returning my texts a few days later. He was graduating soon, so I only saw him one other time on campus. And even then, he was with another guy. That was my second semester.

Outside the Middle Eastern man's room, the young me takes my hand and wants to go to the steam room to cruise for more guys. But I stop, press him against the wall, and my lips go into his hard. I'm about twenty pounds lighter than me-now, so I pick him up a bit, press my body into myself to keep him elevated. I can tell when he wants to stop, so I do. There's almost no light in the hallway, but I still see a glimmer of my eyes. They're wet.

"You don't have to rebound like this," I tell myself.

He sighs deep, and preps himself for what he wants to say, but I cup his cheek and say, "Shhh! You won't even remember him after a few years."

"Yeah, *you* can say that now," he says. "But it was yesterday. He could barely even look at me."

"You look at me," I say and crane my neck to meet him in his eyes. "What's the other part of the question?"

"What question?"

"Do you love yourself?"

He rolls my eyes at me.

"The first one's gut level," I say. "But the second one is deeper than that, right?"

"Right."

"'Do you love yourself, even when no one's around?'"

He nods but I don't believe him. Back in my room, he goes down on me and our mouths are both hot and wet. He picks up a rhythm, faster and faster, but I try to slow him down.

"Take a hit," I say to myself, passing the poppers. My skin dazzles when he breathes it in and then gets really into me. Every breath in feels full of particles in my lungs.

A month later, in St Louis, in the outdoor bathhouse pool, I teach me some fingering techniques I've picked up over time while six or seven guys jerk off to us. Both of me cum like a waterfall's first impact onto to a bed of rocks. He starts to swim away from me so I grab for his arm, but he slips out of it. He walks straight inside, I don't even bother to pick up the poppers and our towels by the side of the pool. I follow myself into the steam room and sit next me in a nook behind the door. I touch my/his elbow and he/me flinches.

"What's wrong?" I ask myself.

"No boyfriends. None?"

"You don't want to know." I say, "that's like spoiler alerts or something."

"So no one sticks around?" He says to me, "you're 35."

"I know our ages."

He narrows his eyes at me. The steam sucks out of the room as someone opens the door to leave. They apparently didn't want to hear this and kill their boner. I let out a sigh and plop my hands down on my legs. I'm wet so it makes a louder smack than I meant to.

"So you just give up. That's what you end up doing? Life gets hard and you—"he mimics me, slapping his own legs. I wish I could tell myself to grow up. Instead, I put my hand on my shoulder. He squirms, but I grip him.

"You don't need to know who it's gonna be. Who's gonna dump you, who won't call you back, who'll cheat on you or who you'll cheat on." I see myself pique at the cheating comment.

"Really?" He says.

"There's a third part of the question, isn't there?" I try to move him off-topic.

"You should know."

"Then tell me so I'll remember."

He lets out a quick groan and furrows his brow, like I do when I'm thinking. Then he gets up.

"I'll show you," he says. He steps out of the nook in the steam room and places his hands on the first guy who walks by. Half these men wouldn't look twice at me. But 19 me...

They start kissing, this random guy and myself. I step in to stroke my back, grab a bit at my butt. But he/me stops me. He turns to me and points to the dark corner of the steam room.

"You sit there," he says. "And watch."

I watch myself go in hard, tonguing this guy and then sliding down to take in his dick. We're both hard, but at first I don't want to be. I want to be there, touching me. But I settle for touching myself.

At first I/he shoots me wry, passive aggressive glances. The guy he's sucking off is oblivious. I'm self-conscious, jerking off to me. Watching me watching me. I close my eyes and let my shoulders fall. I think, "to hell with me." My breathing slows, and I get a rhythm going. A few minutes later, I feel lips touching mine. They're not mine, though. These lip kiss rougher, like there's urgency in the stream room. I open my eyes and it's the guy younger me was sucking off. His face takes up most of my view so I can't see my other self. I give up on guessing whether he's still in the stream room with me.

I make it through Chicago and Baltimore without going to bathhouses. But I walk the streets at night, hoping to run into myself and knowing full well how ridiculous that sounds. In Baltimore, I have drinks with a guy I think I would like. He's got smart-people's glasses and talks in nerdy pop culture references I half-understand. He reminds me of me.

I take him back to my hotel room and the clothes come off. He's just objectively better looking than Right Now Me. He exercises and probably eats right. But he stares at my body like I do at me in the bathhouse, filled with wonder.

We fuck and then cuddle after. He turns the TV on, but I want to talk.

I ask, "Would you ever, if let's say, you walk into a bar and you find yourself, an exact clone replica of yourself. He looks just like you, he is you. Would you ever?"

"That old question. Would you fuck yourself?"

"It's stupid."

He says, "I bet if you try the fabric of the universe would fall apart right before it happened. Like space and time would rip. You'd tear yourselves apart."

"That's too," I search for the words, "that's too quantum physics. I guess I'm asking before all that. Just you, in a bar, with yourself."

"Would I fuck myself?"

"Would you love yourself?"

He fumbles over the bed to fetch his glasses off the night stand. Then he takes a deep breath, thinking over it, and says, "no."

"No?"

"That's not the kind of love that's healthy, I don't think. In fact, isn't that just narcissism?"

"No. It's—"

"How many gay couples have you seen that are basically walking twin sets of each

other?"

"Sure."

"If I was attracted to someone who looked like me, I wouldn't be in bed with you right now."

"Okay, ouch."

"Why is that 'ouch'? Show me where it hurts, and I'll make you feel better."

"All right, let's stop talking about it."

"About hypothetical situations of hypothetically fucking our clones? Yeah, let's move on."

I study this guy for a second, stare down from his 5 o'clock shadow to his small, tight torso. He's darker skinned than me, like how I hope I'd look every summer, instead of just sunburned.

"I bet it's easy for you," I say. "You can walk into a bar and turn heads."

"And you think you can't, but you did. You got my head's attention." He laughs at his own joke.

"You don't get it."

"Yeah, I don't get that after: three beers, a conversation where I was checking you out and dropping hints more than actually listening to you, and some solid, grade A hotel sex, you want me to call you ugly?"

I close my eyes for a second to steady myself and see a flashes from back of my eyelids of bathhouses.

I say, "I want you to admit that it's hard for me."

He looks down at his crouch and says, "nope. Nothing's hard anymore." Then he rolls out of bed to get dressed. While he's stepping into his skinny jeans, he says, "you know what? You're the type of guy that I actually look for. But, you, you're too stuck in your own head."

The last trade show of the summer is in Cleveland, which is also home to the country's largest gay bathhouse. I research it online. Three floors, one of the largest jacuzzis in the country. They have a bar and a restaurant, a porn theater, a rooftop beach. The first day of the trade show whips by, which is good. I start to find that I can't think or speak clearly with my clothes on anymore. That suddenly the collars of my button-downs choke me and my dress slacks start to feel like cages around the mid-thigh. Fully dressed, I play a version of myself, and no one seems to catch on that I'm a bad actor.

I settle into my room on the basement level of Cleveland's bathhouse. This one's got a full-sized bed, sheets and pillows. There's an end-table and a TV, not propped up to the wall, but on an entertainment stand. It's like a real hotel room.

I strip out and put my towel on. There's a steam room maze, and I check there for myself. I'm not there; I'm not in the jacuzzi, or any one of the three saunas. Right outside the porn theater, where there's already a group of men getting started, is the rooftop beach. In Cleveland. I step out, walk to one of the corners. I can almost see the lake past the tops of buildings. It's a deep blue and it feels not quite like the ocean—all the wind without all the salt.

I'm naked, three floors up from the cars passing by, but they can't see me anyway. I breathe deep, let the wind wrap over me, when I hear him. It's just like me, but on playback. I turn around and see myself, younger, thinner, sprawled out naked on a lounge chair, sipping a drink and laughing at some older man's comments.

He doesn't see me walk up. I stand in a direction that casts my shadow over his face.

"Yo! My sun." He says before he realizes I'm him. "I don't want to talk."

"Who says we have to?"

He eyes me up and down and a slow grin creeps across his face. I want to not feel like I'm high whenever he/I checks me/him out, but I can't; we have a hold on each other. I want to fuck me, but I also want to squeeze my arms around me and melt. I want to take me outside of the bathhouse, even if it's just once. But I also know, somehow, that's not possible.

He grabs me by the hand, takes me down the outside stairs to the heated outdoor pool just off the patio of the bathhouse bar. He kisses me in short pecks, once or twice as we dip into the pool. I try to put my arms around his shoulders, but he slips out into the water.

"You said we didn't have to talk." He says.

"We don't."

He splashes me. Then swims up to me. We kiss and the world swirls like every other time we kiss. But this time he dunks my head underwater. My nose feels like it takes in a flood of chlorine. I open my eyes but only see the water-distorted version of me looking back on myself. My eyes burn. I push up, break the lip of water and heave for oxygen. I see myself laugh, at myself. I've gone flaccid and finally catch a glimpse of myself for what I actually look like to the outside world: a nineteen year old boy who can't process his feelings.

I get up, out of the pool, and walk inside, past all the dry naked men, drinking beers and flirting. The water on my skin is already cold by the time I make it through the hallway and into the large room with the indoor pool, jacuzzi and showers. I go for the showers first. Get my head wet and warm up.

I could leave, right now. Finish the trade show, go home. Next summer I can go back to hotel bar fantasies and force myself to talk in suits until it feels normal again. I bend my head up to face the stream of water.

"I don't know what I'm doing." I hear. I shake beads of water from my head and see me at the edge of the tile floor, standing in the entryway to the showers.

"I don't either." I tell me.

"But you should, by now at least."

"Well, I don't!" I yell at me. "Sorry!"

He squints his eyes, he's thinking, about me.

"We grew up." I say, "but that doesn't mean everything gets solved. You. You're."

"I'm what?"

"You're not going to get fixed by someone. No one's going to swoop in and make you feel whole. The best you're ever gonna get, is me!" I turn the shower off and just stand there, naked in front of myself. You'll never feel more naked than standing bare ass in front of you sixteen years ago. When you're taunt and thinner. When you had more adventure in you and less responsibilities. When your heart breaks one time and it feels like the end of the world, instead of the new normal that you are now. I don't have anything left for myself.

He takes four quiet steps up to me. His eyes focus on my new hairline, the one that happens in front of you but you still don't see it. He touches my stomach, which I'm not sucking in, looks down at the flesh of it. We meet in our eyes. My first impulse is to kiss me, but I stop. He puts a finger on my bottom lip, and then one on his. He kisses me with his fingers still on our lips. But it's a kiss I can't remember. It's like a single piano note stretched out. His hands move like a glacier to hold me—the first time he's/I've ever done it.

I hear him say, "you're room?" But he only actually says it with my eyes. I lock the door and he climbs on the bed, my bottle of Super Rush sits on the nightstand. I knock it off with one hand, grab him to kiss me with the other but he stops. He wiggles out from underneath me, picks the poppers off the floor and cups his hands around it.

"I'm not gonna make you do them," I tell me.

"No. I'm going to make you." He says, twisting the cap off and bringing the rim to my nose. One deep breath in, then another. The fumes reach into my brain and reconfigure it. One more deep breath in, then another.

We fuck each other for over an hour. No foreplay, just us inside each other in as many combinations and positions we can think of. It's mostly silent save for a few light moans, grunts, and the slaps of our sweat-wet bodies flopping against each other. When I top me, it feels like a forceful act of mercy. Almost religious, and when he tops me it feels like some kind of return. I invite his/my dick inside me the way I'd invite memories into my mind walking through my parents' old home again.

And when we hit the poppers, so many times that our nostrils dry out from the fumes, their sudden rush throws me into his body. Not just literal, not just a spiritual meeting of two essentially the same bodies. The vapors swirl us together like a river of time across space. To the point that, when we cum together, I'm alone. But also, whole.

Denial Twist

Your first night at a gay bar is the sum total of every nightmare you've ever had. Your parents are dead, you're naked, everyone's speaking French and your teeth are falling out in slow motion. You see him through the parts of bare-chested male bodies in the crowd. His pink afro wig is studded with glitter. He brings the cigarette from his lipsticked mouth down to his side where smoke lingers around his cut-off jeans. He's a head taller than everyone else around him so he spots you with your arms huddled around your chest looking at everyone but trying not to, looking at him but trying not to. It's too late, he saunters up to you.

"Drink?" he asks.

"No thanks," you say. "Gotta drive home."

He pulls up a chair next to you, crossing his furry pale legs. "That means you can buy me one."

You laugh at how forward he is, say, "okay," and make your way to the bar. The barely eighteen year old bartender in a g-string asks what you're having and you suggest anything fruity. When you come back to the table he's already halfway through another drink and buzzing off—literally, flying his flat hand in the air—the random guy who took your seat while you were gone.

"I don't take candy from strangers," he tells you. "I'm Andy."

You tell him your name and he places a hand out, like a lady at court. "Enchante."

Up close you can see Andy's silver eye shadow and fake lashes, you can also see his five o'clock stubble.

"I do pose for pictures," he says, rolling back his shoulders and pointing his toes.

"What?"

"Staring! You're staring."

"Oh. I'm sorry."

"Don't worry, darling. It's your first night here."

"How did—" you start but the flick of Andy's eye and his up-turned eyebrow stops you dead.

Andy's not so much convincing as he is demanding and after ten minutes you're already two beers in. The Vanity Fair of club kids commence and you meet the so-called everyone: Ricky, Ben, Rafe, Adam, Sean, Patrick, Mark, Lee and Jamieson. They're gay club avatars, complete with tight shirts, highlights and tattoos.

Andy says it's time to switch to hard liquor and you start drinking Long Islands. Half an hour later when you stand up to leave your body damn near topples over. Andy offers to walk you to your car and once you're outside and around the corner he pushes you against a wall. His mouth comes onto yours and his lips massage yours open. The alcohol swimming around your brain shuts down perimeter defenses and Andy's tongue gets in your mouth, moving your tongue around. Ten seconds later and you're moving your tongue against his in your first wet open-mouth dance.

You're back at the gay bar by sundown the next day.

When you dream, Andy takes the form of some Medusa woman with sparkling snakes weaving out of his wigs. In some of these he has woman's breasts and rocks his stomach in fluid belly-dancer waves. This isn't too far from reality. Andy's a half-drag gay club goddess, merciful with liquor and undivided attention and then ruthless with insults and banshee laughs of superiority.

He only kisses you when no one's looking, behind dumpsters and in unlit corners. Sometimes his press-on nails slip under your shirt and his fingers feel his way around your chest. Andy talks about all the men he's dated but you can't form the mental picture of him and anyone, you included.

One night you and Andy pull up to the parking lot at the same time. You park next to each other and get out just as a group of young guys come out from the corner.

"Hello boys," Andy says.

"How much is the cover to get in?" One of them asks.

"It's free," Andy says. You see one guy trade his glance from you to Andy, and then back.

"Uh, what kind of bar is this exactly?" He asks.

"It's gay, sweetie!" Andy yells. He's already drunk. Andy locks his arm into yours and you start off walking toward the front door.

"So, you're fags!" The kid says. Andy just lifts his free hand in the air and twirls his fingers. Then you hear a sharp gust of wind and Andy's suddenly on the ground. You turn around just in time for your face to connect with another kid's fist. You crane over but don't fall.

"Fucking faggots," yells another kid. Two of them stand over Andy, kicking him. You grab one by the shirt and throw him to the ground. You don't have time to think about how you've never actually punched someone. You take a quick step back for balance, close your fist and land it into the kid kicking Andy. Bouncers show up to clear the rest of them. No one calls the police.

That night Andy comes back to your apartment. For the first time, you see him in clear lighting. His right eye's red and swollen. Dirt from the parking lot streaks across his cheek and blends into his side-burns. You kiss him anyway, slow and long. Your fingers cross welts on his chest as you take his shirt off but he doesn't wince. When Andy lies back on your bed, bare-chested and bruised, light and shadows bounce and hide around his pec muscles and abs. You take a moment to breathe in this new Andy and that night, for the first time, you feel a man inside you.

Andy's not there when you wake up. The bed's just filled with you and dirty condoms.

You start going out to the bar even on weeknights and Andy's a no-show. He doesn't answer your phone calls. Without him around the club kid parade won't talk to you, but you see them look as they whisper gossip back and forth to each other.

Weeks go by, and then you see his car in the club parking lot. Andy's in the driver seat with a sheer green wig, bent over. You get close enough to see him wipe his nose and then blot his lipstick with a napkin. He sees you and just waves. Inside, Andy's too busy catching up with everyone to talk to you. You have to buy your own Long Islands. Andy and his boys go in and out of the bathroom in groups of three or four. They come out wide-eyed and loud, tapping their fingers against the bar, laughing or fiddling with napkins.

Around one in the morning, you tell Andy you're heading out and motion to the door.

He says, "bye, bitch."

The next weekend at the bar, Andy doesn't even acknowledge you.

Two months go by and you watch Andy slim down. You know all the bouncers and bartenders by name now. Jimmy, the bartender your age, slips his phone number to you once on the back of receipt paper, but you still look at Andy, coming in and out of bathrooms, pretending to be on his phone when he sits hunched over inside his car in the parking lot.

You find him outside one night, not too far from where it happened.

"We need to talk, Andy," you say and he turns around.

"Oh, it's you."

"Why are you doing this to yourself?"

"Doing what?" He laughs and you search his face for something, some kind of facial tic that maybe cuts through to the inside of him. "Wait," he says. "You think because I fucked you once that we're something."

He's drunk. He waves his limp hand in a bridge between you two and laughs more.

"I just think maybe you should talk about, you know, what happened?"

"What happened?" Andy smiles and even in the dim parking lot glow you can see specks of white powder under his nostril. "I got beat up, that's what happened."

"Andy—"

"I get beat up, big fucking deal! Look at me."

Andy's lost about twenty pounds since you've known him. The fibers of his tank top cascade over the humps of his ribcage. His muscles have disappeared.

"Well, let's talk about it," you say to him as he teeters back and then steadies his balance.

"Let's talk about it!" He screams and steps closer to you. "You know, I recognized those boys. I did. I suck their dicks when their girlfriends won't. Those boys, and you, you blow up my phone."

He belches, "I get beat up 'cuz I'm a fucking queer. And then I get fucked up. And you liked it, huh? You liked saving my day? Are you my white knight?" He roars laughing at this.

"You have a problem, Andy."

"And it looks surprisingly like you. Now, you're standing between me and the bar."

You step aside so he can stumble through, but then go back to your car and go home. You're not out at the bar for a few weeks. Andy forgets all about you when you do come back. After a few months, Andy's skin and bones, and then he's just gone. For a half-drag gay club goddess, no one seems to care about what happened to him. No one, but you.

A Step Toward Evolution

Because I'm dramatic, the first thing I do when I get back from the clinic is vomit. I haven't eaten much though, so it's mostly stomach acid, burning all the way through my throat and into the toilet. I grab a towel, wipe my mouth and it hits me that the towel's got microscopic gonorrhea all over it now. I drop the towel in the toilet and the fibers expand soaking up toilet bowl water. And this is the moment everything shifts.

If this were a movie, this part would be a freeze frame. I'd stop in mid-motion and a voice over of my own voice would talk about how I got gonorrhea-of-the-throat in the first place. But this isn't a movie. So instead I break out my clippers and shave my head down to the guard. It's faster than I realize, and now I'm almost bald. If I keep this up, I can be in Orlando by nightfall.

I grab one of my roommates awful drum-n-bass mix CDs, and then I grab his car keys.

* * *

We met at a job interview. Neither one of us got the job, but he offered to get coffee when we were both done. He wore a suit like he was testifying in court. Made him look stiff and nervous, but even still, suits always shape a man in that where I want to imagine the man underneath naked.

* * *

My cell phone rings through half the drive, then, thankfully, dies. I remember Orlando like a childhood board game, so I don't need GPS to guide me. I roll into the parking lot of Revolutions. It's still early enough in the night that the parking lot has a few extra spots.

The doorman doesn't remember me so I get carded, but one of the bartenders does so I get a shot quickly. The first bar in Revolutions has a wrap-around VIP section of booths, so everyone not-big-time has to sit at the bar. My legs jackhammer against the bar stool and a patron notices.

"I want what you're on." He smiles at me. He's gotta be two decades older than me.

"I don't think you do." I tell him and laugh to myself.

* * *

One night he took me out to a nice restaurant in Baldwin Park to meet "an old friend of his." He sat across from me and the old friend was running late. When The Friend comes in, white and skinny, he shivered even though we're in Florida. He sputtered something about being nervous, me meeting his friend.

We got drinking but didn't order food. Then my boyfriend told me he's leaving me for this guy. That they've been seeing each other for almost a year. That whatever-the-fuck name this guy has was engaged to some woman, but broke it off last week. He'll get excommunicated for it, but they're in love so who cares.

"I know this is a lot, Donny. But I'm tired of hiding and I'm tired of faking being happy. I'm ready for something real. You understand, right?"

* * *

I'll settle for the guy he left me for, but I really want him. I perk up every time someone walks in. Search their faces and then mentally discard them. My brain's moving faster than my body—that's why my leg is jerking, to keep up. But I realize for just a glimmer of a second that I don't have a plan either way this could go.

I've got three days and today's Thursday. The lady at the clinic said seventy-two hours after the shot but it's better to wait a week. She said that part condescendingly because she was judging me.

"If you practice safe sex, then how did you end up here?"

When I get back I want to try to get her fired.

The music kicks up now, gay thumpa-thumpa. And the lights get lower. Even if I can't see their faces outright, I'm sure I'll know them by how they walk, their mannerisms.

The old man slides a bar stool closer to me, and says, "guess he's not coming?"

"I literally don't know."

"I've been stood up once or twice before. Sure, you could keep waiting. Or you can make the best of your night."

This is technically the first person I've talked to since I got diagnosed and treated this morning. I almost want to blurt it out to him. But maybe he'll earn it.

"What's the best my night'll get?" I ask him.

He goes straight for my ear lobe, cups it between his fingers, and says, "what is someone like you, huh, Egyptian?"

This guy is promising. I put up five fingers and say, "I'm mixed. Guess."

Middle Eastern is not one, so the thumb goes down. He gets Black so the index stays up. Misses with Cuban, but keeps going down the Latino road and until he craps out. I give him a peck on the cheek—not enough to put him in danger. But if I run into him again and he says something racist, I'll blow him in the bathroom and he can figure out his situation later.

* * *

I ran into The Friend two weeks after I got dumped. I decided for a straight bar, a place no one I know would see me, so I could get plastered in peace. But there he was, playing foosball with a bunch of his buddies. Guess that excommunication thing didn't pan out. Fucker.

When he saw me he stopped playing, patted every one of his guy friends on the back and motioned toward me. Then he perched up next to me at the bar.

"I am so sorry, bro." He said, and I wished my pint wasn't half empty.
"Okay."

"I want you to know that. I, no one, meant for this to happen. I mean, I fought it. Hard."
"Okay."

"I know you've gotta be super mad right now. And I know, I'm like the last face you ever want to look at but I'm here tonight if you want to talk."
"Okay."

"'Okay.' You keep saying that but are you? Are you okay, bro?"
"I'm not your bro." I tried to keep going but my throat clapped.

"Dude, if you gotta get it out, just go for it. I'll tell you what." He gets up from his stool and stands close to me. "Hit me. You can hit me. Like, I don't know, seven times."

I'd been monologuing to myself for two weeks, about what'd I say if/when I ran into my ex again. I watched enough prestige cable television shows to know how I'd deliver it. Where to pick my voice up so random passersby would know something's going on. How to work out when to breathe to accent the right combination of words to drive it all home. I had it all queued up for the ex, but never thought about The Friend. I closed out my tab and found another bar.

* * *

I pick a spot on the edge of the dance floor so I get a good view of the room. All these white men swish to some beat that I can't hear; I at least follow the music. I let myself get lost in the beat, the strobe lights, and the alcohol for just one second and a raging cough catches in my lungs. I almost double over, two degrees shy from choking. My vision gets crystallized seizing for air. I watch the strobe lights bounce off the reflective panels of the dance floor. Time almost stands still, but then I do catch a good deep breath and get whipped back into fast motion again.

I step out to the back patio to smoke a cigarette and like a sculpture that moves out of the corner of my eye, he's there.

I don't have time to figure out whether I want him to see me or not. He spots me right off, calls my name and waves me over. He's sitting on a bench with a young Black guy.

"Donny, it's been forever," he says, then he leans closer to the Black guy. "We used to date right after college." He offers me a seat but I don't take it. "I just met this handsome guy, tonight. Donny, this is…"

"Ricky," he says with a sharp point. He's not impressed with me.

"It's been a while," I tell him.

"You in town visiting?"

"Only for a few days."

"Can we go? This place sucks." Ricky says.

"Yeah, I'll leave you two to it." I say. I want to ask him if he still drives that red Buick, if he still lives off Semoran, what his work schedule is like tomorrow and where he'll be over the weekend. But instead I just turn around and leave. He catches up to me though, and apologizes for Ricky.

"Do you want to grab coffee while you're down here? I'd love to catch up."

"Sure, I don't have the same number anymore."

He pulls out his phone and I take it from his hands. I search through his contacts for my old number, but I'm not in there. I throw him a wry look. I add myself and text me: "coffee."

"You look good, Donny."

I give him a once over. It's been four years and he doesn't look any different. He might even be wearing one of the button-downs I bought him. The only way I can tell the years have gone by are in the corners of his hairline.

"Thanks." I say.

They leave and I stay. I keep dancing and drinking. I try to advertise myself like a victim looking for a vampire, but most of the white men are only interested in each other. And most of the men of color are obsessing over the white men. I twerk, drop it on the dance floor and the night whips by without anyone talking to me.

I get a room at the Holiday Inn downtown and slide in drunk, thinking about all the blow jobs that must have happened here. I stumble into the bathroom to look at myself drunk in the mirror. It's a fun game I played in college, to study my face drunk, see if I'm different. My cheeks are a deep reddish brown, flush, and my eyelids are heavy. The seconds still run by like a sped-up metronome.

* * *

We had five dates before anything moved past kissing. We drove out to New Smyrna Beach on our 5th date and watched the families play with inner-tubes and build sandcastles. He put his arm around my shoulder and I tried to nestle myself onto his chest. But my legs weren't quite settled right and I ached after a few seconds. Every time I tried to shift, he'd squeeze me tighter, to keep me where I was.

He talked about wanting a family someday, if marriage gets possible. And when he described the fictional kids in his mind, I knew they were lily-haired white children. But feeling his chest lift and cave with the tugs of his heartbeat pulsing out of him, I accepted the dream. He talked about always feeling like he had to be the good boy, for his mom and siblings. How everyone from his backwater Florida hometown was expecting him to "make it."

Back in his car we kiss and then he stops me.

"Do you want to see my Good Boy?" He asked.

My lips peeled back into a smile and when he let loose his pants, I dove in for him.

He whispered, "yes, you like that Good Boy, don't you?"

* * *

I cough through my sleep, dreaming of that Good Boy now.

In the morning, my phone's fully charged. Buried in between

voicemails and text messages from my roommate are a few from him. Great seeing me, let's do coffee today. He texts me the address to a Starbucks on University Blvd.

He wears polo shirts now. I'm guessing he just walks into Ralph Lauren and buys what's on the mannequin. He gives me a kiss on the cheek and I suppress a cough.

"So did you make a night of it with Ricky?" I ask him.

"I don't want to talk about that." He says, "I want to hear about you and Savannah. Do you still play music?"

"Yeah, and I teach, obviously."

He grabs his cup of coffee and says, "I guess it's not obvious. I haven't seen you in four years."

"Well," I say, "you didn't leave things in a 'let's keep in touch' kind of way."

"Damnit," he says, "can I just say, I was a fucking idiot. I don't want to dwell on that, but, goddamn that was a mistake."

"No, this was half the reason we're getting coffee." I say, "I want to hear all about it!"

He takes a deep breath and my eyes widen. I hang for words like "break up," "left me," and "done now." But that's not what I hear. Fellowship, missionary, South America, Anthropology.

"You're still together." I piece the words out.

"He hasn't been in the states for more than two months in the last two years."

"You're married?" I guess. I sip my coffee and eye for the Starbucks exit. Gonorrhea was supposed to be the cherry on top of his sad, single life. Picking up insecure Black and brown guys needing that special kind of white validation. Thankfully, time moves faster now. I stop myself and think to wait.

"So what brings you down here?" He asks.

"Nothing really, just wanted a weekend away."

"Everything's okay there?"

I pounce on this moment and lie. I'm fantastic! I make up a boyfriend who resembles the guy who gave me gonorrhea.

"He didn't come down with you?"

"No," I say, "he trusts me. Sometimes you just need a solo trip. Go where you've been before."

"Where are you going tonight?"

"I mean it's Friday. I'll probably end up at the Parliament House."

"I've got to get back to work, but maybe I'll see you there."

He flashes that smile I remember from our second date. It's the kind of smile that tells me he's thirsty, but he won't act on it. I make it back to my hotel and check out so I can check into the Parliament House. I don't have to wonder about illicit blow jobs in Parliament House rooms, they're part of the history. They go back to the 60s.

I have another coughing fit and rush to the bathroom in case I have to vomit. But nothing happens. I sit on the thought, gripping the hotel toilet. Nothing. Being nothing.

* * *

Once, we got into a fight in a liquor store. There was some guy giving out free samples of whiskey and he offered everyone but me. My boyfriend takes the shot, flirts a little, but I was still stood there, hand out. I clear my throat to make myself known. And the whiskey guy pours a half a shot less than he did for my boyfriend.

"Whoa," I said. "That's not much."

"I didn't know if you were drinking," the whiskey guy said.

"I'm in a liquor store."

"All I know is Never Forget."

"What?"

My boyfriend stepped in, "baby, let's go."

"No, I don't understand."

My boyfriend tried to say it in a low whisper, "It's September 12th!"

"Yeah. Two thousand and fucking fourteen!"

My boyfriend tugged my arm, but I didn't budge. "I'm sorry," I say, "is this some white holiday now?"

"If you don't like America, go back to your desert country," the whiskey man thinks I look Arab.

"Baby," said the boyfriend, "let's just leave."

"I. Predate. You." I told the whiskey man. "You think you own this because you bought it in blood? Your people wrapped our children in smallpox blankets, to exterminate us."

"Wait, I thought you were black, Donny."

I took the half shot of whiskey and slapped the tiny, empty plastic cup on the display counter. It was too small to have the impact I wanted it to.

"I'll meet you in the car." I told my boyfriend.

There, we got into it.

"That's not how you fight racism." He told me.

"Don't fucking tell me how to pick my fights."

"But you're not helping your—"

"Who the fuck am I supposed to be helping? You?" He tried to speak but I cut him off. "September 12th! Like it didn't happen to me too."

"Even I didn't know you were Native American."

"You never fucking asked! What? Am I a double exotic now? Not your average Black dick?"

"You're really upset."

"And you aren't! He told me to go back to my own fucking country! And you just stood there. September 12th. You know what, fuck you."

"Hey, I didn't do anything."

"Exactly!"

He left me for a white man three months later.

* * *

I feel the bass of the Parliament House dance floor through my hotel room windows. I chug a deep swig of rum and cough on it. This is another part—if my life were a movie—where we'd freeze-frame. I'd say something poetic, and destructive. But instead I go out in the club complex and pick up any man who'll have me.

I blow strangers, full throat, and the time speeds up so I lose track of how many. The first few, I would rinse my mouth out with water, but then I stop doing that. Fuck them.

I'm in the courtyard when an arm slips around my shoulder. He squeezes me, but I wince.

"I'm glad I ran into you."

"I got a room here. You know, why not?"

"Whoa," he says to me. He studies me like I'm somehow different, after all these years.

We get shots and beer in the courtyard, dance in the club, I smoke cigarettes outside and he watches me.

"I don't mind the smoking," he says to me.

"I don't care."

"Well, that's harsh."

"I'm supposed to be nice?"

"No, but you seem drunk."

I decide not to banter with him. I lean back against the brick wall behind me and take a long drag on the cigarette. The coughs feel like they're getting less and less.

"I know you hate me," he says. He wants me to say something back, so I don't.

"But, can we be real? What kind of life would we have had together? Not, like, the money or bullshit society, us?"

"We would have had domestic flights," I say, and then smile.

"I really hurt you," He says. I try to lift myself up off the wall, but he's right, I am drunk. I scrunch my face at him, like I'm trying to say something profound and closure-y. But I'm lying with my whole body now.

"Nobody hurts more than another, right? It's all the same hurt. And we surface it, bring it to each other."

"You're drunk."

He takes me back to my hotel room, and I hear him lock the door behind him.

"Oh, you got liquor here," he says, noticing my handle of rum.

"Fuck you, I'm on vacation."

I try to keep lying with my body. Like, how does a happy drunk stand?

"Take your clothes off, Donny." He says.

"No, let's play a game," I say and hold up five fingers, "guess?"

"I can't remember."

"You can't remember or you didn't ever know?"

He frowns for a second, eyes the door. So, I switch it up.

"Here's the score, you guess right, I take something off. Guess wrong, you take something off."

"This isn't fair. You know the answers."

"Guess."

He says Black and my shirt comes off. Then he says Asian, which is too broad, so I make him narrow it down. He gets Filipino wrong and takes off his pants. He's naked before I can finish my fingers. He slides himself up the hotel room bed, his Good Boy hanging out. I crawl like a big game cat on top of him.

"Wait, no, you're Indian!"

"You already lost."

"You're Native American, I remember."

"You remember? You remember this?" I take his dick deep into my mouth and it stiffens as I get a rhythm. I push my throat on him like I have no sense of self-preservation. He moans. I've only got a day left so I flip him over to make extra sure. Shove my tongue between his cheeks. He loves it. He begs to fuck me, but the transfer doesn't work that way. I move up to kiss his face so deeply my lips are inside his. I cough once, just slightly, right into his mouth.

* * *

After Obama got re-elected we spent all day in bed. He studied the dip in my back like he had a magnifying glass, but still somehow, needed to get two inches close it it. Then he stopped.

"I could stay in bed with you all day."

"Mmm," I said. "But tonight my friend's performing. And I've told everyone about you. We're going right?"

"Uh, do we have to? I just want to lounge around. It's a weekday."

"I want you to meet my friends."

"I will."

"But not today?"

"Don't be mad, Donny." He rolled off me and pull my arm up to move me closer to him. My arm stung, but I didn't say anything. "We have all the time in the world, to meet our friends, our families. We don't have to rush it."

"It's been a year and a half," I said, "people want to meet you. I want to meet your people."

"But you don't really. Just trust me," he says and bear hugs me to lift me up closer to him.

"I love you," I said, even though the bulk of my arm was caught underneath him, and prickling, and going numb, and, finally, silently dying out.

"I know you do, Donny."

* * *

In the morning, the few strands of light that slip past the closed curtain windows picks up the two mounds of his gleaming white ass. We fell asleep last night right on top of the hotel bedding, not even bothering to cover ourselves. This is a Parliament House hotel room so anything you could imagine two or more men doing to each other has probably already happened on this bed.

Still asleep, he drapes his arm over my chest, tugs his hand in just below my ribs, and pulls me in closer to him. Except I don't want to, and for the first time probably ever, I stiffen my body against him. I dig the heels of my feet into the mattress and roll my shoulders back so my chest puffs out and expands. He's still asleep and he grips harder onto me, tugs harder. He sleep moans something that sounds like a muffled no, and then it happens. Through the crisp, thin sunlight beaming into the stale hotel room that still smells like man-sweat and booze, he coughs. It's just a few tufts of air at first. His fingers are still bent around my side. But as the cough takes hold, he lifts his arm off of me and wakes up.

Come Clean

Me, Mama, and Joel rent movies almost every night. After school if we do our homework in time Mama'll drive us to Hattie's Hut where they have almost everything. Takes a while to find something we can all watch because Joel's a worse scared-y cat than me; he even gets scared of movie box covers. There can't be nothing that looks even half dark on the front picture or Joel'll start to whimper. We stick with Pixar.

Watching *Up* Joel freaks out in the first thirty minutes, when the doberman still has that deep voice, and he runs to the bathroom. He locks the door and we can hear 'em crying. Mama takes the movie back to get something hand-drawn-animated and tells me talk him down. A song works and he usually likes anything Beyonce. If anyone at school could see me I'd be dead, singing Single Ladies to a eight year old on the other side of the bathroom door. Get through the whole song twice and I can still hear crying. I switch up to anybody else I know and go through most the whole radio this week when the phone rings.

We don't answer when Mama's not home but it won't stop. Rings three times, stops and rings again so I pick it up.

"This Julius?" Says the voice of the phone. It's an old man, sounds fat.

"Yessum."

"Now I don't want to upset you none. This is Sheriff Crawford. Your ma's been in an accident. Now how old are you, boy?"

"Twelve."

"And little Joey?"

"Joel. He's eight."

"Do you got aunts or uncles or none?"

"In Claxton." I say, "Mama says that's a drive."

"You got their phone numbers?"

"Uh huh."

"Give 'em to me."

I do. Then the sheriff says, "I'm gon' send a squad car to pick you up. Your Ma's at Good Faith Hospital. Now, you boys mind him, okay? I'm gonna call your auntie."

The officer's name is Mr. Braker but he says I can call 'em Charlie. He can't talk Joel out the bathroom any more than I can and he finally gets through the lock with a debit card. I tell Joel about Mama and he stops the crying noise, guessing now he's really scared. So am I but I'm the big brother so I can't let it show.

We get to Good Faith and Charlie takes us all the way to Mama's room. The doctors tell us she's fine to our faces but I can hear bits and pieces of what they say to each other. Something about attack and having to use victim kits. Joel keeps it cool til he sees Mama in the bed asleep with tubes and things coming out of her. He cries out and then runs into the hospital room bathroom and clicks the door. I don't wanna sing to him around all these cops and nurses so I just say, "Joel, please don't. Not now, Joel," and I start crying too.

Aunt Tae shows up and talks to doctors and cops. The cops talk to me to get all the details of the night down but I don't know nothing they don't and they know more than me since they keep whispering. I don't hear what happened til Aunt Tae tells us in the car.

"Some man." She starts, but her voice quivers all up and down, "I guess he acted like his car was broke. It was on the side of the road. He hurt your mama, hurt her real bad."

"Is she gonna be okay?" I ask.

"Your mama's a strong woman, Julius. But they got a lot of work on her."

Joel starts heaving.

"Don't y'all be afraid, now. I'm gonna stay with you through this. Take you to school in the morning and take you both to see your mama every day, okay now?"

Aunt Tae tells us not to tell nobody at school what happened but all the kids know somehow. My classmates bob and weave out my way in the halls. My math tutor gulps when he sees me.

Mama's in and out of it when we see her after school. She hates the lights when she's awake and raises her arm to block the glare. That's when I see bandages on the inside of her arms, three of them each.

Mama doesn't remember any of what happened but she twitches like crazy in her sleep and sometimes wakes up screaming. Some days she keeps telling me and Joel she's sorry, sorry for leaving us at home to go to the video store, sorry we have to see her this way, and other days she's mad yelling at us for being scared-y cat boys. Either way, Mama makes Joel upset and he stands in the doorway or against the wall, trying to be as far from her as possible.

Aunt Tae won't tell us any more than some man hurt Mama and I try to ask about her bandages, where's she hurt at and why doctors kept talking about kits that first night; Aunt Tae won't say nothing. The three of us eat dinner in quiet at home and sometimes Aunt Tae can't handle it. Everybody's on ups and downs: Mama, Joel and Aunt Tae, going from "just fine" to "can't take it." I tuck Joel into bed every night.

"Why'd that man hurt Mama, Julius? She didn't do nothing to 'em." Joel asks.

"I don't know. Some people are just bad."

"Is Mama mad at me?" He asks, "cause I get scared?"

"No, Joel. You know Mama loves us."

"Do you still get scared?"

I want to tell the truth, that I do all the time and especially nowadays. I want someone to throw my fears onto and tell me everything will be okay. But Aunt Tae won't answer any questions, Mama's in and out at the hospital and Joel's just a boy still. Being the big brother's lonely.

"I don't get scared no more." I tell him, "And when you get bigger you won't either. Trust me on it."

Aunt Tae brings Mama home from the hospital while we're at school and she spends the whole day sleeping. Aunt Tae says she's still healing so she'll be tired a lot and we gotta be mindful. Mama won't come out of her room til the sun goes down and Joel tries to show her the card he made for her at school but it's one of her bad days and she tells Joel to just leave her alone. Her eyes narrow watching Joel trail head-down to his room. When she sees that I see the way she's looking at him Mama yells at me.

"Get your eyes off of me, Julius, so help me!"

Aunt Tae and Mama stay up at night talking and I hear little bits of it. Aunt Tae says to let up on us, that we're scared and she needs to talk about it. Just saying the word "it" throws Mama off and she either cries or screams. Mama takes to throwing things too, and I clean up the broken plates or glass in the morning while Mama's sleeping.

Mama only used to scream at us when we acted out real bad, but she's different now. One night I hear her say as much to Aunt Tae.

"I'm changing. What happened changed me and I can't stop it."

"I know, Sis." Aunt Tae says.

"No! You don't! You don't know. You don't know what it's like to have this evil in you now. And I never asked for it! I thought I could do right to help someone out. So fucking stupid!"

I never heard Mama cuss. Hearing it now makes my spine sink like a brick on top of my mattress. I feel like I can't move, like I'm trapped and I have to clench and unclench my fists just to keep myself breathing. Mama never cussed and the F word sounds like so much hate coming out of her. And I want to grab onto someone and squeeze 'em til I fall asleep but the only person who used to let me do that was Mama and Mama's not Mama no more. I'm scared of her and can't tell nobody about it.

Every night I overhear more and more of Aunt Tae and Mama talking about her changes. I ask Joel once, after we get dropped off at school if he hears them talking at night but he says no and he's glad he doesn't.

"I don't like hearing Mama say anything anymore." Joel says.

All the girls in my class read those *Twilight* books and talk about vampires and how much they wish they could meet one and I almost speak up to them. I almost tell them my mama met one and he almost killed her. Instead, I sit on the thought and it makes its own sense after a while. I remember the cop Charlie asking after the man that night at the hospital. They told him Mama said he had dark hair and was white. Mama couldn't give good enough description to the face artist a few days later. He could be anybody, I remember Mama saying.

And Mama doesn't leave her room until after dark and her good days, when she's nice, don't come around anymore. Joel knows to go to bed before Mama gets up because he's afraid of her yelling. But I stay awake in bed and listen to Mama and Aunt Tae. Aunt Tae's the only one who'll talk to Mama and Mama takes advantage of that, laying into her "lifestyle" in Claxton. I can't always make out what they're saying but I can make out the way Aunt Tae's voice pitches up and down, like she wants to cry but is holding it back.

I ask my math tutor about those *Twilight* books.

"Nah, I don't read that stuff." He says, "It's for girls."

"Girls can't turn into vampires?"

"Yeah, they can. In some movies, girl vampires can control any body around them, and make them do things they don't want to do. I saw another vampire movie where this girl turned into a vampire and slept on the ceiling of her room."

"The ceiling?" I ask. Ain't been in Mama's room since she broke all the dinner plates.

"Yeah, cause vampires are like bats sometimes."

"They scream like bats?"

"Sometimes, I guess."

"I don't like those vampire movies."

My tutor laughs, "Yeah, everybody's got their monster that freaks them out. Like, I like vampire movies but I can't stand zombie ones. Something about 'em is just too creepy."

"Zombie's are worse than vampires?"

"I don't know," he says. "You can kill a vampire but zombies are already dead, and they're always in a group. It's that group thing that gets me cuz you can't ever win. You know?"

I know the vampire movies are too much for me but I figure books can't be worse, so I check some out at the school library: *Dracula*, *Vampires in Hollywood*, and *Vampirism: Myths and Lore*. I read 'em in my room at night when Mama comes out and starts on Aunt Tae until they're both screaming at each other. I barely see Mama anymore but when I do she reminds me of the pictures I see in some of the books. Her hair's frizzed out and scraggly; the dark circles she used to have are worse cause she's not getting any sun. These books and Mama's voice give me nightmares. In 'em, Mama's eyes stare at me or Joel through walls and past buildings no matter how far we run from her and she always knows where we are. In my nightmares, Mama's eyes are yellow like in the pictures of the books.

I sweat into my pillow every night, afraid of every noise Mama makes pacing around the house in the dark. In the mornings my hands rattle as I sweep up whatever Mama broke over the night. Maybe it's a big brother thing or a getting older thing or maybe it's just cause of what happened to Mama but I start to think that being scared is how I'm supposed to feel. I don't need to clench and unclench my fists to calm myself down anymore. In fact I don't even need to feel calm anymore. It's not the safety feeling it used to be when I was little and Mama would sing to me before I went to sleep to keep the nightmares from getting me. As long as I'm quiet enough for Mama not to hear me at night, I can have all the fears and nightmares that the darkness can conjure.

One night Aunt Tae comes into my room instead of sitting in the living room waiting for Mama to come out. She says she just needs a few minutes away from her. Then she notices my books.

"You're into vampires? When did that happen?" She asks.

I shrug, "I don't know. It's just something for school anyway."

"Your mama's not well, Julius."

"I know."

"That man really did something to her." I nod, she keeps going, "I can't stay around much longer cause I got a job and people to get back to in Claxton. But I want you to call if your Mama hurts you okay? She needs some help but I don't think she's gonna get it any anytime soon."

We both hear Mama scream out Tae's name. She says, breathing deep, "well, I better go see what it wants."

Aunt Tae creeps out of my room and I stay sitting on the bed thinking about "help" and what Joel and I could do that Aunt Tae can't. I pick my books back up right as Mama starts her yelling again.

Each book says something different about cures. Garlic and coins. I could try killing the man on the road, and then there's the obvious ones I'm too scared to even think through.

Aunt Tae leaves in the morning, after dropping Joel and me off at school. From now we're gonna have to walk to school if Mama won't take us. Neither Joel or I have the courage to ask her. Without anyone around at night to yell at, Mama still screams anyway, and cries, and smashes things. She starts buying red wine from I don't even know where. I collect the bottles every couple of days for recycling.

I try garlic first; hatch up a plan in Social Studies. We don't see Mama eat but she's got to, at least even a little. I wake up super early one morning and make oven-ready lasagna and garlic bread, but I add more garlic to both of them. Then I get Joel ready for school and we leave the meal steaming on the dining room table. Joel wants a quick bite of the bread but I tell him no and we leave for school.

In some of that folklore I read eating garlic's just enough sometimes, especially in Romania. But we don't live there and when I come home from school all of it's splashed on the kitchen floor. I send Joel to his room and scrub the tile with a Brilo pad, praying I can be done before the sunset. I hear Mama breathing in her sleep even though her door's shut.

One book talks about coins in the mouth, to keep the vampire out but there's no way me or Joel could even stand straight enough to walk into Mama's room—even during the day when she's sleeping. My tutor lets me borrow a vampire movie. It's about vampires up in Alaska where the sun doesn't come up for a month. I take the TV into my room and watch it with the volume just low enough to be under Mama's screaming.

These vampires work in groups and they don't stop til they get almost everyone. My right arm and my left leg twitch hard when they turn a little girl and she pretends to be sad so someone will help her. Then she tries to attack, runs around in a store dodging any and everybody. She's got to be head-chopped to stop her and thank God they don't show it. I can't hardly breathe as it is. I go to sleep with back-sweat and leg-sweat and have new nightmares about Mama turning Joel, about Joel screaming and hollering all night long and our house is so cold I can see my breath and there's no more food in the fridge because they don't want it anyway and they want blood. And in the dream I stop running. I can feel my sleeping self push my head into the pillow but I'm still dreaming and saying to myself, nothing works if nothing's broken. Nothing broken, nothing broken. And I'm tired of my family being cracked like this and there's no way away from them. I feel a dream breeze that's heavy and I nod my head against the pillow.

It's no use. And they'll get me anyhow. They both hate me because I'm not like them and in the dream I lay down on the kitchen table and watch the sun cast its light slowly up the wall until it's gone for good. I hear their doors open and their loud breathing and Joel laughing too and so is Mama. And they don't make it fast because they know I'm scared.

Mama slams her arm down on my shoulder joint and Joel jumps up with his tongue open. And I want to open my mouth and scream out for help but it's not that kind of dream and I can't undo the decision I made anyway.

Nothing works if nothing broken, I say. Nothing works if nothing's broken.

I wake up on my back, my arms and legs spread out on the bed. At first I don't even recognize my room, I just stare up at the ceiling until I remember it's Tuesday and my name's Julius. I even forget to be scared.

I don't shower or brush my teeth. Instead I empty bed sheets from the linen closet and grab a pair of scissors to cut 'em up into long vertical strips. Joel wakes up and wants breakfast but I tell him no and have him help me with this.

"We're not gonna be scared of Mama no more, Joel. You hear me?"

He nods, staring at me but I don't think he really gets it.

"It's about being in groups," I say, collecting up all the bed sheet strips. "Groups always win. You can't out last 'em."

I take Joel's hand and we step slow toward Mama's room. She's breathing loud and deep on the other side of the door. Joel tries to slip his hand out of my grip but I squeeze on tighter.

"No!" Joel says, and his eyes start up.

"I told you one day you'd get bigger and you wouldn't be afraid anymore. Remember? I told you to trust me."

"Uh huh."

"We're gon' make that day today. And then, starting tomorrow we won't be scared of nothing, all right?"

I throw the sheet strips over my shoulder and turn the knob on Mama's door real slow so it doesn't make noise. Then I inch the door open. First thing I do when I look in is to check the ceiling but Mama's not up there, which is good. That would've just made things harder. The air in her room's colder than the rest of the house and it feels like it ripples my skin when I cross the doorway, dragging Joel behind me.

There're more wine bottles and broken plates all over the room. Me and Joel tip-toe around them. I give him a few strips and tell him to tie her legs down to the bedpost. He says no at first but I shoot him the look like Mama used to when he'd done bad.

"Quiet-like." I mouth-whisper to him.

It helps that Mama sprawled out on the bed and that she sleeps like the dead now. We've never waken her in the mornings. I tie two sheets around each of her wrists, make sure they're real tight, and then check on Joel's work and help him out a bit.

Mama's breathing sounds like those Alaskans. I find a piece of glass with a sharp edge and then grab Joel. Mama doesn't have bandages on her arms anymore, but you can see the scars where that man did what he did. I bring the glass up to one of them and press it into Mama's skin.

She wakes up right away, screaming. Mama tugs her arms and legs but we've got her too tight and she can't move. I push Joel's head into Mama's arm where blood's coming out and he tries to push back away.

"Drink it, Joel!" I tell him, which gets Mama's attention. The skin under her eyes collects in puffy mounds and she screams straight at us. She doesn't brush her teeth anymore and they're yellow even in the dim light and her breath smells like foul garbage, like a dead animal.

"Drink it!" I tell Joel again.

"No!" Mama screams. "Fuck! Fuck! Fuck! Fuck! No!"

"Don't listen to Mama, just drink!" I say.

"Piece of shit kids! You're dead!"

I run to the other side of the bed with the glass shard and cut into Mama's other arm. I see Joel take a few gulps and then cough a bit. He steps back from Mama with blood on his mouth.

Mama screams out the F word again as I cut and a stream of red comes out of her arm.

"It was your fault!" She yells at us, "You stupid fucking scared-y asses!"

I put my mouth up to Mama's cut and suck in the blood. There's a metal taste to it that I almost gag on. It collects inside my mouth as I fight against the gag for one big swallow and feel the blood fall down my throat. None of the books or the movies are precise on how much you need so I go back to Mama's arm for more. Joel's tugging on his stomach and crawls over to the far wall away from Mama, who's screaming about hating us, hating our different daddies, not wanting us anymore. I try not to listen; girl vampires can take control of people. I get three more mouthfuls of Mama's blood when it finally hits my stomach too and buckle over. My insides seize up and then calm down then seize up again, but I'm no stranger to ups and downs anymore. These must be the changes Mama told Aunt Tae about.

Mama screams herself hoarse and whimpers and bleeds on the bed and both me and Joel are on the ground, shaking and holding our guts in our hands. I see Joel on the other side of the room, past all the broken fragments of Mama's things. His back's stuttering like he could be crying real hard or laughing. Then my stomach really has at it with the blood. My body wants to throw it up but I hold back against it. I think about how the changes'll be different now, that it's all of us at the same time. Think about how the dark and shadows won't upset Joel anymore, how I'll never be scared of anybody because they'll all be scared of me, scared of us. And we can go up to Claxton and bring Aunt Tae into our group, too.

The blood starts to make me sleepy and roll out onto the floor. I can't see Joel anymore and instead stare up to the ceiling. Life as a monster up there, it's not so bad because I have Joel and Mama with me now. We all get to feel the same things, together at the same time. I hear sound coming from Joel's side of the room but sleep and nightmares are about to take me. He's either crying hard or laughing. I decide he's laughing.

I wake up just as the sunset starts to slip purples and yellows into the room. Joel's not on the far side anymore, he's right next to me. His brown eyes are as round as the outline of his head. He's not crying or blinking, just staring, waiting on me.

I hear Mama. She cries like the sound of hiccups, short bursts in no kind of set timing.

"Julius?" Mama asks, like she knew somehow I woke up, smelt the change in the air. "Julius?"

"Yes, Mama."

"Come up here, Julius."

But me and Joel just lay on the floor, still. I can't move, part of my brain doesn't want me to.

She says it again, "come up here, Julius."

My stomach feels like I swallowed a brick and it settled down deep between my hips. Other than that I don't feel nothing. The books don't tell you how the changes feel and the movies don't either.

"It hurts." I tell Mama. Joel nods his head slow.

"Untie me and I can help you where it hurts." But I still don't move. Outside, all the colors in the sky thicken and get darker. I thought I'd sense it, the night coming on, but I don't. Just take it in through the eyes.

"Julius," Mama says. "Talk to me. Can you just talk to me?"

My throat's dry, from the blood. Talking's hard.

"It hurts, Mama."

"I know, baby. Mama hurts too."

"It's the changing that hurts, isn't it? That's what it means, right?"

I hear Mama take a deep breath, then say, "No, it's not that."

"What hurts is that you didn't ask for it. That someone made you. Forced you. Like this, Julius, like being tied down. And that's all they do. Some people, they're just evil enough to redesign you in minutes."

"That man on the road?" I ask her even though I know that's who she's talking about, that vampire.

"His car was pulled to the side of the road, like he'd lost someone in the sticks. Had a flashlight, was calling out a name."

Before all this, I'd expect Joel to start up with the noises, tears and all, but not now. All he does is stare. Joel's eyes are so dark brown too that you can't tell the iris from the pupil. I get lost in them.

"He had extra flashlights, said something about a young girl, and tossed one to me. And that was it. I marched. Right out there in the thick. I didn't get a good look at him because he came up from behind."

I can't help but picture this. I remember the way Mama's face strained looking for me in the crowd of other kids at school, back when she used to pick me up, before she started working. I can see that strain-face on her out in the dark, stepping lightly, scanning the flashlight over the tops of grass. I see that man float up behind her, fangs bared, eyes whited out.

"I come to on the ground. I'm face up. He got my hands spread above my head and held down. Does it all with one hand. The other one had the knife."

I'm still looking through my brain's eyes. Mama with the man on the road and he's biting her. The other parts Mama's telling me, somehow, fly off like dust from a flatbed truck.

"Julius?" Mama says.

"Huh?"

"Wake Joel."

"He is already."

"You both listening?"

I say "yeah" twice, one for me and one for Joel, but I don't mean mine. I hear things at school about what I know is coming next. About how sometimes men do things to women. Ugly things. Sometimes to children and little girls. And then someone always has to make that joke about how whichever who did this stuff got a rise out of it. It's not really a joke, actually, just a stressing on that word, rise. Men and boys have that way of saying just one word but it gets to the core of you, because of your body. And then girls at school start to look at you different, like hunger or like terror, and you know that, too, is about your body.

"He did something to me, you understand boys?" Mama says, "Like punching and like stabbing but worse." Mama licks her lips, then continues, "He violated me."

I'm not even sure Joel comprehends anything. His little chest rises and falls and I think he could lay down silent for twelve years. But I'm shattered. I see that vampire fold away in the air like dead leaves. What's left is just a white man with his pants down, on top of my mother, getting a rise out of it. It hits me in what's left of my stomach, how that white man broke us all that night. And that I've been so afraid that I, I let the night take over.

Afterward

After the election of Donald Trump, denouncing identity politics has become *de rigeur* in liberal circles, even as white nationalists – who explicitly practice the most nativist and genocidal form of white identity politics – have grown exponentially in terms of power, visibility and legitimacy. Well-meaning liberals continue to tell racialized people that the only way forward is to make space for *both sides*, that tolerance mandates we care about the feelings and desires of people who have vowed to kill us. Diversity, apparently, doesn't only mean diversity from whiteness: white supremacist thought is, in this historical moment, a "diversity of opinion" too long missing from the discourse in the public sphere. In this imaginary, white nationalists become just another kind of *minority*: another iteration of difference that must be tolerated.

What does a literature for this era feel like; what can it hope to accomplish after decades of circular postmodern reasoning and an abandonment of the idea that Truth with a capital T can still be collectively possible? What can fiction say that hasn't already been said before?

The stories in Reuben Hayslitt's collection do not provide answers to these questions, because to ask these questions is to already step over and elide the mess of incoherence that is our waking life today. These stories are not concerned with providing a way forward – they are grappling instead with what it means to make sense of a quagmire that cannot be made sense of. In other words, these stories are as messy, complicated and knotted as the times that have produced them.

In a seminal 1975 text, Deleuze & Guattari situate "minor" literature as the only literature capable of being great.[1] Minor literature – the inflection on *minority* is intentional – is literature that refuses to be governed by dominant codes of interpretation; a literature that insists that the whole story is always escaping our grasp; a literature that works to move the final meaning of a narrative away from and in order to unravel the "centre" of the story. The multiple hyphenated *minor* identities occupied by many of the narrators and characters in this collection continuously shift our attention away from the centre and towards somewhere else. Each story unravels in one way or another, formalistically or narrativistically – the centre doesn't always hold. Hayslitt confounds our expectations at every turn, conjuring and then stepping over the line between realism and magical thinking, between fiction and science fiction. There are no genre distinctions here, only genres confusing into and melding with each other.

The stories in this collection, written before and during the 2016 election, function as a kind of lodestar. They are not explicitly political, but politics hover unmistakeably in and through all of them. They are not realist, but realism pervades even their most magical elements. This is their abiding strength.

Asam Ahmad
September, 2018

---

[1] Deleuze, Gilles and Guattari, Felix, *Kafka: Toward a Minor Literature*. Paris: Les éditions de Minuit, 1975.

Past Titles

Running Wild Stories Anthology, Volume 1

Running Wild Anthology of Novellas, Volume 1

Jersey Diner by Lisa Diane Kastner

Magic Forgotten by Jack Hillman

The Kidnapped by Dwight L. Wilson

Running Wild Stories Anthology, Volume 2

Running Wild Novella Anthology, Volume 2, Part 1

Running Wild Novella Anthology, Volume 2, Part 2

Running Wild Stories Anthology, Volume 3

Running Wild's Best of 2017, AWP Special Edition

Build Your Music Career From Scratch, Second Edition by Andrae Alexander

Writers Resist: Anthology 2018 with featured editors Sara Marchant and Kit-Bacon Gressitt

Magic Forbidden by Jack Hillman

Frontal Matter: Glue Gone Wild by Suzanne Samples

Upcoming Titles

Running Wild Stories Anthology, Volume 4
Open My Eyes by Tommy Hahn
Legendary by Amelia Kibbie
Running Wild Press, Best of 2018
Running Wild Novella Anthology, Volume 3
Surviving Childhood Slavery by Robert Shafer
Christine, Released by E. Burke

Running Wild Press publishes stories that cross genres with great stories and writing. Our team consists of:

Lisa Diane Kastner, Founder and Executive Editor
Barbara Lockwood, Editor
Cecile Serruf, Editor
Jenna Faccenda, Public Relations
Rachael Angelo, Business Relationship Developer
Tone Milazzo, Podcast Interviewer Extraordinnaire
Amrita Raman, Project Manager
Lisa Montagne, Director of Education

Learn more about us and our stories at www.runningwildpress.com

Loved this story and want more? Follow us at
www.runningwildpress.com, www.facebook.com/runningwildpress, on
Twitter @lisadkastner @JadeBlackwater @RunWildBooks

CPSIA information can be obtained
at www.ICGtesting.com
Printed in the USA
LVHW041755190919
631611LV00013B/1273